About the Author

Lexie Winston has been an astronaut, rock star, princess and time traveller. In her dreams. But none of the dreams have lived up to what becoming an author has been like. She gets to live in a world of pure imagination, and her heroines get to do the things she's always wished she could.

When not writing books, Lexie is a mother of two gorgeous teenagers and the wife to a patient and understanding man. They live in Western Australia and are lorded over by a black toy poodle. She loves camping, reading and if her iPad was stolen, her world would explode. (It has the kindle app on it.)

And check out my website at lexiewinston.com

And you can find all my links at
https://linktr.ee/LexieWinston

Also by Lexie Winston

The Collectors Division

(Reverse Harem Series)

Guardian

Guardian's Blood

Guardian Ascending

Neighpalm Industries Collective

(Enemies to Lovers Reverse Harem)

Abandoned Girl

Broken Girl

Tormented Girl

Wanted Girl

Cherished Girl

Loved Girl

Superficial Girl - Jacinta's Story

Seductive Sins Collection

(Reverse Harem Series)

Glorious Gluttony

Gangs, Guns, and Glory

Galaxy Circus

(Sci-Fi Reverse Harem Series)

Apprentice

Stagehand

Whisperer

A Night Most Wicked - Galaxy Circus Novella

Broken Promises

(Dark Poly Romance Series)

Secrets Kept

Lies Untold

M.I.T.H.O.S

(Contemporary RH)

Spies Like Me

Coming 2022

LOVED GIRL

LEXIE WINSTON

NEIGHPALM PUBLISHING

First published by Neighpalm Publishing in 2022

Loved Girl: Neighpalm Industries Collective

Mobi format: 978-0-6450988-8-4
Print: 978-0-6450988-9-1

Cover design by Breakout Designs
Edited by Inked Imagination

 Created with Vellum

To unexpected wins!!

Chapter One

Thomas

The taxi weaves in and out of traffic as I look at the watch on my wrist and curse. I had tried to rush through all the things I needed to do last night so I could get to the ship earlier than I had planned, but it hadn't worked out that way. And now I was running even later.

Max had begged for me to help her, and I could hardly say no to her. She's Harlow's best friend, practically her sister, and at one stage in our teens, we were all pretty close too. When Chuck and Melinda would come out to visit, Max enjoyed hanging out with us guys as much as she did Jacinta. It wasn't in a weird she-wanted-to-get-in-one-of-our-pants way; it was just like having a cousin. I had made the arrangements she asked for, so the plane was available to take her where she needed to go. She didn't tell me exactly what she was running from, but I know it has something to do with the three men who couldn't take their eyes off of her at the gala. Their background checks might help give me some kind of clue, but until those come back, I'm at a loss.

I don't feel bad about snooping. Even without Dad's friendship with her parents, Harlow's connection to Max makes her family. We always look out for family.

The taxi pulls into the drop-off area, interrupting my mental recap of how I got to this point. I throw some cash at the man and burst out the door, carrying my bag. Whether there's change, I have no idea, nor do I care. It feels like forever since I've seen Harlow, so that's my priority. Hurrying through all the waiting people, I try to find the right ship, but then I hear a person call my name. I stop, spinning around, trying to see if it's me they want or another Thomas, and my heart sinks when I see Kai waving me down.

"Oh, thank god I caught you!" The words rush out of his mouth as he stops in front of me.

"What are you doing here? Why didn't you call me on my cell?" I ask him, frowning when he looks at me like I'm an idiot.

"Because I knew you would see it was from me and ignore it until you had gotten settled on the ship."

I won't bother denying it because it's the truth. "What's so important that you couldn't wait?"

"Forrest called. He said he's been trying to reach you. Veronica must have gotten sick of waiting because she followed through on her threat. She tried to commit suicide last night."

A jolt of fear brings a rush of goosebumps to my skin. "Fuck, the baby?" I ask, putting my bag on the ground and pulling my phone out of my pocket. Sure enough, there are a couple of missed calls from Forrest. I had switched my phone to silent mode for the ball and hadn't switched it back on yet.

"She and the baby are both fine. It was a fairly tame attempt, not that that description makes it feel any less alarming. They think it was for attention, more than anything, but the doctors want to speak to us, and it can't wait."

My gaze swings around to the three big ships in front of me. I don't want to leave Harlow, but she has Jaxon and Jacinta with her, so at least she's not alone. Not to mention that security on board have been alerted to the situation and are under orders to keep an eye out for anyone behaving suspiciously around Harlow.

Kai must see my indecision because he's quick to jump in with reassurance. "She'll be fine. She's got the twins, and we'll let them know not to let her out of their sight. In fact, it's probably best if she's not allowed to go outside—even on the deck."

I still don't love it, but then I remember the look on Harlow's face when we were talking before the gala. This baby isn't just some kind of responsibility that we're being saddled with. This baby is the start of a family for us, Harlow included, and I know she'd want us to prioritize making sure it's in the safest conditions possible. Even if that means talking to Veronica instead of cuddling up with her. The two of us start walking back to the drop-off area, where he's illegally parked. After my bag is shoved into the back of the SUV, we climb in while I try calling Jaxon.

His phone rings, but it goes to voicemail, which would normally have those first hints of panic stirring, but now is not the time for that. I try to remind myself that I've got systems in place to protect them, and at this point, Harlow and the others know better than to take unnecessary risks. Jaxon was so excited about this new venture, I'm sure he's probably just watching the boarding procedure.

"Jax, it's me. Something has come up, and I'm not going to make it. Make sure you two don't let Harlow out of your sight. I want someone with her at all times. The likelihood that the stalker is on the ship is slim, but I don't want any of you taking risks. And yes, even when she goes to the bathroom. If she's annoyed, she can call me later and yell at me. Have fun and stay safe."

Hanging up, I shove my phone back into my

pocket as Kai directs the car toward the mental facility that Veronica was apparently moved to after they stabilized her.

"We couldn't have done this over the phone?" I ask my brother, unable to contain my annoyance.

"No, they insisted on a face-to-face meeting. The theory is that she'll escalate until she gets the kind of attention she wants, and speaking to her over the phone would probably just give her another excuse to try something more drastic until we dragged ourselves in there." Kai sounds as annoyed as I am, so it's not really fair to take my anger out on him. His grip on the steering wheel is white knuckled, and he's tapping one finger in a repeated pattern.

This is definitely more than just annoyance. Fuck, I'm being selfish. Although it's not an ideal situation, I know Kai is fully committed to being a father to this baby, and he must be worried out of his mind. I resign myself to holding back as best I can, at least when I'm talking with Kai.

When we get there, we're led to a conference room. There we find Forrest, who introduces us to two doctors and the prison warden. I guess his vacation must be on the back burner for the moment. Hopefully this won't take too long, so he and his wife can get back to it as soon as possible.

"Thank you for coming, Thomas. I know I had other plans today," Forrest says as we take a seat. "These are Dr. Wiseman, Veronica's medical physician, Dr. Reed, the psychiatrist in charge of her case, and Warden Ellis. They've asked you here so we can discuss Veronica with you both."

"What about her? She really is none of our concern," I ask them, my irritation reigniting. Wasting time on this devious bitch when I was supposed to be relaxing and getting some much-needed time to work on my relationship with Harlow is basically my worst case scenario right now. It's a little hard to separate and compartmentalize my feelings about her even though I know they're separate from the feelings that I will develop for the baby.

"No, but that baby she carries is, and it would be in your best interest to hear the doctors out," Forrest scolds me, and I sigh.

"I apologize for my tone. At this very moment, I was supposed to be heading out to sea with my girlfriend to drink and eat and spend some quality time with one another without too many distractions," I say to the gathered men.

The two doctors look sympathetic, but the warden just looks annoyed. "Can we get on with this? I've got places to be," he grumbles.

Dr. Wiseman nods and takes the lead. "As you have been informed, Veronica made an attempt on her life yesterday, though we feel it was a half-hearted one at best. She used her bed sheet, fashioning it into a noose, but she hadn't really even secured it to anything. We believe it was more for attention than to do any real damage. "

Dr. Reed takes over, looking directly at me. "She seems to have had a break in reality. She believes the two of you are in a relationship and are planning to get married."

My brother and I exchange a glance as he sighs. "That couldn't be any further from the truth. I'm not sure if you have been informed about how she came to be pregnant with my baby…" He trails off when the doctors nod their heads, their expressions as disgusted as they should be. "Look, I will love that baby with everything I have, but any kind feelings I may have had toward Veronica have been annihilated with her actions." They exchange another glance.

"See, there lies the problem. She's in denial and won't hear what we tell her about it being *your* baby. She insists that the baby is Thomas'," Dr. Reed says quietly. "She also says that if we don't produce Thomas, she will do everything she can to kill the baby. I don't like it any more than you do, but it's not like we can restrain her for the next four months until the baby is born. Right now, we're all well aware that she's manipulating the situation, but our hands are tied. All we can do is find the best solution to our current problem. Really, Kai, I hate to be so frank, but it doesn't quite matter how you do or don't feel about her. With her interest so focused on your brother, he's the one we need to buy into this strategy."

My stomach feels like there's a lead balloon in it, and Kai looks positively green. Forrest takes over because he can see we're both at a loss for words.

"What is it you want from us? How can my clients possibly help?"

"We believe it would be in the baby's best interest for Thomas to pretend that he's willing to go along with her demands. If you agree with this, we'll tell her that her placement was done at your request because you wanted her and the baby to have the best care, that the six-month in-hospital program is her best shot at you two having a future together. That would hopefully be a useful first step to getting her to calm down. We will try not to push you too far, but at a minimum, we'd like it if you could visit during any prenatal appointments and encourage her because her contact with the outside world will be limited while she's in the program."

"Is that even legal for us to manipulate her like this? As her doctors, you're allowed to arrange this?" Kai asks, glancing between the two doctors with skepticism on his face. Honestly, I'm not surprised that it is. The doctors' priority is to provide for her physical and mental well-being, and if the harsh truth would completely undermine and threaten that, well, I fully believe they could justify this course of "treatment."

"She kind of loses all rights because of the

crime she committed. It's either here or a maximum-security prison, which may shatter her already
fragile mental health. She may never see the inside
of a maximum-security prison. We will reassess her
after the baby is born and taken from her custody.
This could all just be a clever ploy to keep herself
out of jail," Dr. Reed informs us.

"And how does that help me?" Kai says, immediately jumping back in. "I want to be there for my
baby's appointments."

"I don't see any problem with you being at the
appointments. We'll just tell her you're there to offer
moral support for your brother. " Dr. Wiseman
shrugs like what they're suggesting is no big deal,
but I feel ill at the thought of getting close to her
like this.

"Are you basically implying that if I don't do
this, our baby won't make it?" I ask him, the feeling
of dread growing with every word out of these
men's mouths.

"Yes. Essentially, she doesn't see the baby as
anything but a means to get what she wants. She
shows no maternal instinct whatsoever. In fact, in
one of our sessions while I was assessing her mental
capacity to go to trial, she suggested that the baby
would have a nanny and go to boarding school. If
you wanted your child to have siblings, then a surrogate would need to be employed because she wasn't
risking her figure again.'" I'm not sure if I appreciate the matter-of-fact way that he's sharing this,

but there's an undercurrent of disgust that at least makes me feel like he understands our position.

"Basically, she got what she wanted from the pregnancy because she believes that it's her ticket into the Summers family. The baby is a means to an end, and even though deep down she knows she's in trouble for what she did to her roommate, she's going to use this baby for as long as possible," Dr. Wiseman warns us.

"But what about when she gets closer to giving birth and her delusions are coming to an end? What's to stop her from blackmailing the Summers further?" Forrest points out even though I know what I'm going to do. I'll do everything to protect that baby, even if I have to pretend with Veronica.

"Veronica has demanded a Caesarian for the birth, so we will be able to schedule a date for it," Dr. Wiseman informs us. "Because of her incarceration, she loses all rights to the baby, which gives Kai full custody. There will be nothing to blackmail the Summers with. Once that child is delivered, it will no longer be anywhere near her."

"Okay, I'll do it," I tell them before either doctor can say more, "but I refuse to do *anything* physical with her. Additionally, the visits will be restricted to when she has prenatal appointments, and Kai will be with me."

"We will be petitioning the court not to allow Veronica any rights to the child—even supervised visitation—in the event of her actually leaving this prison one day." Forrest pulls out a document. "But if she would be willing to sign over her rights to us, that would be better and certainly easier."

"Maybe Thomas can convince her to sign it. Tell her that you don't want the baby taking her focus away from you, and she will probably jump at it. Appeal to the narcissistic side to her, and she won't even hesitate. Tell her that she's so special to you, you can't stand to share her with anyone else, even the baby. The nannies can have the baby while she remains solely yours. That should ensure her cooperation, though I really doubt a court wouldn't grant you full rights anyway. Either Veronica really is mentally unstable, or she's a criminal who is being charged with attempted murder. No judge in their right mind would ever allow her to have access to her child," Dr. Wiseman suggests.

I sigh, standing up and grabbing hold of the piece of paper. "Stay here. I'll go speak to her. Maybe the doctors can go over the results from her latest baby scans with you while you're waiting," I tell my brother. He doesn't look happy with the idea, but thankfully, he doesn't argue with me.

Dr. Reed stands up and gestures for me to follow him. "I'll take you to where she's being held, and Dr. Wiseman can stay here." He leads me out of the conference room and through the facility until we stop in front of a door.

"She's restrained for now, and she'll probably beg you to release her. We've told her we're still not convinced she's not a danger to herself and the baby, so you won't have to worry about her throwing herself at you. There are multiple ways to handle this, but given her state, I believe a firmer approach would be best. We might have a better outcome if you act angry at her for what she tried to do and unsure how committed she is to your 'relationship.' Until she can prove herself by not harming herself, then you're not sure if you can commit to her as well." He sighs and runs a hand through his hair, looking slightly defeated for a moment. "I know it's manipulative and deceitful, but I'm not sure what else will work for her. Appealing to her good nature won't because I'm not sure she has one. If she was willing to go as far as to poison her roommate to further her ambitions, there's not much else to stop her."

"Let's get this over with," I growl, not hiding the anger in my voice. I'm not angry with the doctor so much as the situation, but he's receiving the brunt of my feelings.

He opens the door to a small windowless medical room. The artificial light makes Veronica look washed out and sickly, but her eyes light up when she catches sight of me.

"Thomas, you came!" she cries with joy and struggles to sit up even though she can't. She frowns at the restraints on her hands.

I just stare at her, hoping my disgust doesn't show on my face. I'm not sure I can do this, but I guess they can't keep her restrained for the whole pregnancy.

"Hello, Veronica," I say calmly, and she smiles.

"Where have you been? I've been asking for you! Did you hear that we're having a boy?" I look at the doctor, and he sighs.

"No, Veronica, we told you you're having a girl," the doctor says firmly, but she doesn't even look away from me.

"I was thinking about Thomas Jr. for his name, so we can call him Tommy," she gushes, and I can feel my blood pressure rising. This is either an academy-award-winning performance, or the girl really has cracked.

"Well, we won't be calling him anything if you keep doing what you did," I growl, unable to make my tone nicer. She flinches, and tears well in her eyes.

"But how else was I supposed to get you to visit me?"

"Veronica, the doctor has insisted that this facility is the best place for you so that you can work on your mental health so that you can be the best mother—"

She interrupts. "And wife?"

"Well, to be honest, I'm not sure that you're cut out for it," I tell her. Beside me, the doctor flinches, but I'm pretty sure I've got her figured out. "If not seeing me for a couple of days is enough to set you on a path of self-destruction, what's going to happen if we get together and I'm away for weeks at a time, or when the press is following you everywhere, watching your every move?"

"Oh no, I would be fine! I promise," she begs, her eyes shiny with hope.

"The best thing for you to do would be the in-patient program so that you can take care of yourself and keep our baby healthy. I'll start interviewing nannies and register him with the finest of Swiss boarding schools for when he's old enough, but I need you to promise me you will do everything they ask." My nausea rises with each of the words coming out of my mouth, but I keep telling myself that it's necessary.

"Yes, anything." She smiles widely, so I nod for the doctor to remove her restraints.

"And there's one more thing. I need you to sign this paperwork." The doctor unclips the buckles, releasing her hands, and she grabs for the paper and pen. Not even looking at it, she signs away any parental rights, and I breathe a sigh of relief. Halfway there.

"Excellent," I tell her as she looks to me for approval. Normally, I would feel guilty about manipulating someone like this, but she's done so much worse to Kai and myself, not to mention her roommate. "I'll return for your next visit with the obstetrician, and Kai will be coming to support us as family. I expect to find you healthy, and I want you to try to eat a little more. I don't want our baby boy to be underweight. I know a fantastic surgeon who can always give you a little nip and tuck once he's born."

"Oh, that would be lovely," she simpers, which is about all I can take. I step back when she holds her arms out for a hug, and her face falls. *For the baby, Tom. Do it for the baby.*

Gritting my teeth, I step forward and embrace her quickly, feeling her thin body under my hands, before stepping away. I'll do this for my brother and the baby, but I won't give her any moment longer than necessary for their sake.

"Work hard to please the doctors, and I will bring you something next time. Don't disappoint me, Veronica." After that, I hurry out, leaving the doctor behind to deal with her. I rush in the direction of the bathroom, passing Kai without a word, and push through the door. It's by the grace of a step that I make it into the cubicle in time to lose what little I had in my stomach.

When I come out, my brother is standing there with an open bottle of water, his eyebrows turned down in a frown.

"I'm sorry, man. This is fucked." He hands me the water and leans against the wall as I rinse out my mouth.

"It is, but I will do anything to keep our baby safe, even if I have to pretend. I've worked out that she likes all the attention on her. If I can distract her with shiny things for the next five months, we might come out of this relatively unscathed."

"Harlow is going to be pissed." He scrubs a hand through his longer hair, and we both leave the bathroom, walking back to the conference room.

"Yes, she is," I agree, "but she'll understand."

After I give Forrest the forms so he can do whatever he needs to with them, my brother and I leave the prison facility.

"I know it's early, but I need a drink."

Kai nods. "Let's go back to the hotel. We can drink all day to forget that clusterfuck for the moment, then fall into bed tonight without having to worry the rest of the family. We can tell them all tomorrow."

"Sounds like a plan," I tell him, relieved I'll get a reprieve from all of their questions even if it's just for twenty-four hours.

Chapter Two

Declan

The day after the gala, I'm eating an early breakfast in the restaurant of the hotel when Dad finds me. I look up from my laptop, expecting Molly and Emma to join us any minute, but they're nowhere to be seen.

"Where are the girls?" I ask him, leaning back in my chair.

He takes a sip of his coffee and grimaces. "Neither of them are feeling very well this morning. I wanted to do the right thing and be there for them while they felt so bad, but they shouted at me to get out."

A chuckle comes out before I can stop it. "I wonder if Chuck is having the same problem this morning. Melinda was quite the ringleader last night."

Dad's chuckle rings out with mine. "It's great to have them here, isn't it? We went out to dinner with them before the gala. It will be nice for Emma and Molly to have a friend to navigate the shark-infested waters that are our lives. The press is going to have a field day when they finally realize it's not just you boys in an unconventional relationship. You guys have had all the focus up until now, but someone is bound to notice eventually."

"It's sad that we have to prepare for that kind of thing. The Ninja Starfish story took the heat off us for a while. We just have to hope that when they do find out, someone else fucks up and takes the spotlight away from you."

"So, what are you doing this morning?" Dad nods at the open laptop in front of me.

"Well, after Forrest's announcement that we're expecting a baby girl, I got to thinking about our childhoods and how, despite our advantages, you still made us get summer jobs and learn the businesses from the ground up."

Dad chuckles. "The mailroom was never the same after one of you had worked there for a summer. Once Oliver did his time, they begged me not to let any of you work there anymore. I had to find Jaxon and Jacinta other positions to start with."

"Oh yeah, I remember that. Jacinta was so mad that she had to work the coffee cart, but Jaxon loved the window cleaner job. He loved being outside and up so high."

Dad shudders, looking a little green. "I can't believe I let him do that. All it would have taken is for something to come undone or for him to slip."

"Anyway, it made me realize that our baby and any other future children will eventually need a summer job too, so I was looking to kill two birds with one stone." Dad's brow wrinkles in confusion, so I turn the computer for him to look at. "You know all about Harlow's fascination with abandoned properties. Well, I found this one, and I thought it would be a good project and a great place for our future kids to cut their teeth on."

He scrolls through the listing for the abandoned theme park, and I can practically see the man's business mind kicking into gear.

"Huh, I wonder why it was abandoned."

"I was just researching that when you arrived. From what I could discover, it looks like the owner had a gambling problem. He went to jail because he was using the park as a money laundering front to pay off his debts. He had no family to step up and continue running it, so it's sat empty ever since."

Dad's eyebrows raise. "I'm surprised it was never sold off to pay the debts owed against it."

"Apparently, there weren't any. I guess money laundering pays well. He had paid off everything relating to the park before he went to jail. There's a security company that's supposed to patrol it, but it seems they only go around once a week. I'm not sure what kind of damage has been done to it."

"Why is it on the market now?" Dad leans forward, his curiosity getting the better of him as he scrolls through the listing again.

"The owner is getting out of jail, and he wants to sell it so that he can start a new life. Supposedly, he's reformed and found God." Dad looks as skeptical as I was when the estate agent told me that, but all I can do is shrug. "He wants to move away from California and start over, so the place is on the market. It has been for six months. Even if we low ball our offer, I think he'll take it because it's getting close to his release." He stops on a group of pictures, and his mouth drops open in amazement. "Yeah, I had the same reaction."

The picture shows a large round wooden building with sliding doors that open up to expose an old-fashioned merry go round. It's beautifully carved and painted with wooden animals and ornate scrolling along the poles and the rest of the canopy. There are peacocks and seahorses, lions, tigers, and bears, as well as the traditional horses, but they have horns and wings, turning them into unicorns and pegasus. There's even a dragon. The agent told me that all of the animals had been draped with sheets to protect them, and because the carousel has been protected from the elements— apart from dust and cobwebs—it's in immaculate condition.

"Harlow is going to love that." Dad grins and looks at me. "Let's do it. I've been looking for a new challenge, and that might be exactly what I need. We can get the guys working on that as soon as they're done with the zoo. There's no rush, and we'll need to have the rides and water slides assessed by a professional anyway. How much land is there with it?"

He scrolls back to the specifics and reads through them again.

"Enough that we can add more modern rides while keeping the originals as long as they're in working order," I tell him, excitement really buzzing through my veins now.

"Why hasn't this been snapped up by someone else?" A worried crease develops in the middle of his forehead.

"It's a new listing for the agent, and he always sends me any potential business opportunities that cross his desk, though I haven't been interested in any up until now. He's given me the first look and first chance at refusal."

"Well, let's get the ball rolling. I have a grand-baby who's going to need a business to work in, and what better place for teenagers than an amusement park?" Dad's grin is from ear to ear. His priority has always been about being a good person and under-standing the value of hard work. He's never been one of those fathers who put pressure on his kids to get married and start a family, but the happiness on his face makes it clear that he's ready for this new twist in our lives. "It's going to be so weird having a baby around. I've never done that part of having children before, so Kai won't have any shortage of helpers."

"I hate the way it came about, and I hope Veronica rots in jail for the rest of her life, but I'm excited that we'll be adding to our family. I'm also relieved Harlow took it so well. It can't be easy to think about another woman having Kai's baby."

"I think the fact that she was basically raised by another woman helps. Her mother was no picnic either, so it's easier for her to accept that it's not this baby's fault how it came to be. As I'm sure you've noticed, Harlow has an incredible capacity for love. She's already proven that by how quickly she forgave Jacinta *and* how she's embraced the relationship with you and your brothers despite it being unconventional and newsworthy."

"She certainly has taken it in stride. I'm surprised there haven't been more meltdowns, to be honest," I confide in my father. It's been worrying me that apart from the stalker drama, which is pretty serious in itself, everything seems to be going well. "Shouldn't we have more bumps in the road? I mean, I don't want them, and I'm grateful for the peace we're finding in her... But, Dad, doesn't it just feel like that calm before a storm? We had such a rocky beginning that it feels like we didn't really earn it going so well now."

He sighs and leans back in his chair, the business opportunity forgotten for a moment. "I think every relationship is going to have its ups and downs. You've all been dealing with the stress of her stalker as well as running your businesses and getting to know one another. Give yourself a break and be thankful that it hasn't been too hard. I'm sure that will come, especially with the new business to establish, the count's estate, and a baby. All of your businesses basically run well on their own. It probably wouldn't hurt you all to take a leave of absence for a month or so, so you can concentrate on other things."

"It's just this damn stalker. Not knowing why or who is killing me. I feel so impotent. I think we all do, except maybe Thomas. At least he's working toward keeping her safe. What good are the rest of us? How have we helped get her closer to having a normal life again?"

He leans forward again, an earnest look on his face. "You know, I have a gut feeling this is all coming to a head."

"What makes you think that?" I ask him, a frown on my face, but he shrugs.

"I'm not entirely sure. It's just a feeling. I don't know if it was the unveiling of the count's vault and seeing all those drugs and weapons, or something else."

"But what has that got to do with Harlow?"

Dad shakes his head and rubs his chin. "I don't

know, but I think finding Carmen may work toward solving this. I've been trying to run down some old addresses I had prior to the home invasion, but I'm coming up empty handed."

I'm thinking it over, trying to keep a mental list of who's left in our lives that might wish anyone, particularly Harlow, harm, and I realize that we've forgotten someone who should actively be on our radar. "I don't doubt that Cecelia has something to do with it. Her disappearance is too suspicious." I really need to find a new PI, but I don't really want to put anyone else in danger. Whoever this other stalker is obviously has no qualms about killing off people in their way.

Before Dad can respond, I see a very harassed-looking Chuck hurry into the dining room. His eyes scan the area, and relief smooths his face when he catches sight of us. He detours past the coffee station and holds up a mug toward us. Mine is empty, so I give him a thumbs up, with Dad doing the same. I grin as I watch him fill up three mugs and bring them over to the table. He puts them down and takes a long drink of his before he sits. I'm not sure whether it's the caffeine or our presence, but the tension practically drains out of him.

"Thank fuck, I needed that. Sorry, you both got black. If you need something, you're going to have to get it yourself."

Dad laughs and picks up his mug, gesturing to Chuck in a cheers motion. "This is just fine for me.

I'm sure for many of the same reasons that it's good for you."

Chuck shudders. "For such a small woman, she can pack away the alcohol, but when it comes back up, it's like a scene from *The Exorcist*. We'd been asleep for about an hour when it all started to re-emerge. Thankfully, she made it to the bathroom, so your cleaners won't be needing too much of a bonus. She's finally resting peacefully, but I've got things I need to do today that can't be put off."

"Oh?" Dad asks, and Chuck nods.

"I've got to pick up the horses from the movie set. Josh is going to come with me. Maxine was supposed to help, but she's not flying back with the others today. I was going to ask Harlow if she wanted to come, but she's off on that cruise. She's never done anything like that, so I didn't ask her. She's always been such a sweet girl. I know she'd change her plans in an instant if she thought I needed her help. Maxine's really gotten better as they've grown older, but sometimes I wish Harlow had rubbed off on her a little more."

Dad's eyes light up. "Oh hey, I'll come. I can't remember the last time we did a road trip. Just let me deal with Molly and Emma. I'm sure the two of them would prefer to recover without me around, anyway."

Chuck looks some semblance of alive now, and he perks up even more at Dad's suggestion. "Probably not since before all the kids came into our lives.

Yeah, that would be awesome. I'll let Josh know. The other thing I need to do is interview a couple of new stablehands/trainers. Luke's death was sad, but knowing what I know now, I wish I'd never hired him. As for Peter, who the fuck know's what happened to him. People are so damn irresponsible nowadays." He frowns before going on. "I was using your truck since mine won't be here for another week or two with some of the other horses. DS and Jenny came over on the flight with us and have made themselves at home at the new place."

"How are you settling in?" I ask, and he grins. Chuck's practically the uncle we never had, so he's never excluded any of us kids from conversations. You'd think it would be weird now that I'm dating his surrogate daughter, but it's really not. No weirder than the fact that I'm dating my adopted dad's *actual* daughter.

"Melinda has been so happy about having a house all to ourselves. Even though Max will be staying with us, my parents won't be. The space is a little big for the three of us, but we've been talking about possibly fostering a couple of children. Having Harlow in our lives made up for the devastation Melly felt when she was told she probably wouldn't conceive again, but they're all grown up, and we still have a lot of love to give."

"That sounds awesome, Chuck. If you make even half the difference for a couple of kids like our dad did for us, they will be very lucky." Although my home life was good, and it was only due to my birth parents' deaths that I came to be with Dad, my other siblings weren't so lucky. I make sure I funnel a lot of donations to foster and adoption agencies, just to give back because I've been so fortunate. In the back of my mind, I always had an idea that I'd take that support to the next level by taking in some foster kids of my own.

For a long time, that seemed like a possibility that might never come. But now, with Harlow, it feels like that stage of my life is waiting for me rather than being so far off in the shadows I can barely see it. Once upon a time, I might have been intimidated by that. I mean, how do you know when you're ready to be a dad? But there's something about Harlow that calms me and helps me think beyond myself to what I could be and what I could do for others. Something within me is definitely ready.

Dad quickly drains his coffee and stands up, stretching. "I'm going to get the girls some hangover supplies then go back to the room to check on them."

My phone message alert sounds, so I pull it out of my pocket and read the message. My heart skips a beat at what I see there, and I can't help the "Fuck!" that comes out.

"What's wrong?" Dad asks, instantly alert.

"Veronica tried to commit suicide. Thomas and Kai had to go see her. Apparently, whatever happened requires copious amounts of alcohol. They're headed back here and asked me to meet them at the bar."

"Shit, I guess that means Thomas missed the ship." Dad runs his hands through his hair in frustration.

"Don't stress, Dad. Jacinta and Jaxon know not to let her out of their sight. They'll be fine. We'll give them a call this evening to check in on them. In fact, when they realize Thomas isn't anywhere to be found, they'll probably call us." I try to reassure my father despite the gnawing worry inside my stomach.

"Yeah, Dec's right, Brad. Harlow's a smart girl. She'll be fine," Chuck says even though I can hear that he's trying to convince himself at the same time. "Let's take the hangover dragons some supplies and go get these horses. You need to take your mind off things, and Declan will update you on the Veronica situation once he knows more."

I nod my agreement, and finally, the two of them head in the direction of the gift shop. I put in a call to my real estate agent and get the ball rolling on the amusement park, then close my laptop and head to the bar, ready to distract my brothers from whatever drama has encroached on our world today.

Chapter Three

Holden

"Why the fuck did we agree to do this the day after the gala?" Oli grumbles as we trudge our way up the steps to our new house. Jaxon had given us a key so that we could come and go as we wanted or needed to.

"Because we love our girlfriend and sister and know that they want to start having people in here as soon as they come back from their cruise." I'm trying to appease my boyfriend, but he woke up really grumpy and has done nothing but complain since. I know it's because Harlow's going to be gone for three days; we've all become used to being in one another's pockets. But it will be good practice for when things get back to normal and we're all taking business trips for our individual companies.

It's also nice to take some time out for ourselves, even if it means we're doing it while working.

It gives us some of the one-on-one time that we haven't had much of since we got back together. While I love Harlow, I also love Oli, and I don't want either of them to think I can't love them unless we're all together. Separate time with each of them is definitely needed to re-enforce that.

"Hey, babe, I was just wondering what you want to do when we move into this house." Since we're here, I ask him something that has been playing on my mind for a while. Oli stops in the foyer and turns to look at me.

"What do you mean?"

"Well, I was kind of wondering if you and I would share a room here?" I can't bring myself to look at him in case I see something I won't like in his eyes. "I mean, I know we have our own spaces at Dad's, and we could, I don't know, maybe still have two rooms if that's what you want. We could always make them interconnect, but I was wondering if you wanted to share a bed with me when we move in." The rest of it just rushes out of my mouth. If I don't get it all out, I'm worried I'll chicken out. Our reconnection is just still so new that I'm second guessing my instincts. I think I know what Oli is going to say, but there's always a small chance that it won't be what I want to hear. I just want him to know there's an us even when Harlow isn't around, and I guess I'm hoping he feels the same way.

Oli's quiet for a moment, too quiet really, but suddenly he's rushing at me so quickly I'm unable to brace myself. The two of us go tumbling to the floor, my body cushioning his. The breath rushes out of my lungs, and before I can recover, Oli is covering my face with kisses.

"Yes, yes, yes, *absolutely* yes," he says in between wet kisses. I grab his head in my hands, holding him still, and take his mouth with mine. Brushing my tongue across his lips, I quickly gain entrance. Our tongues stroke together, and Oli's muffled groan makes me want to smile as he grinds his body against mine, but I pull away to look into his gorgeous brown eyes. His glasses are slightly crooked on his face, so I straighten them before brushing another kiss against his mouth. His lips chase mine when I lean back, but I hold him off.

"That makes me really happy, and as much as I'd like to finish this and take care of that..." I grind my hardened length against his. "We can't. We have a lot of things to do." I roll him off me, and he lays on the ground, eyes closed, trying to compose himself as I get to my feet.

"Tease," he grumbles, but he still grabs my hand when I hold it out to him. Once he's on his feet, I smack him on the ass.

"The wait will be worth it," I promise as I pick up the bag I had dropped when he tackled me. I hear a truck coming down the driveway before I can do anything else or even close the front door.

"Oli, take this." I pass him the bag of things I had grabbed from Dad's when the helicopter dropped us off early this morning. "Make us a coffee, and I'll deal with the delivery drivers."

Oliver peers in the bag, and its contents bring a small smile to his lips. "Where did you get that from?" he asks when he sees the drip coffee machine I had placed in there.

"Mrs. Heyton had it in the back of one of the cupboards. It's the one we used to use before we got the fancy machine and became spoiled. I figured it would work until we could get one of our own over here."

He leans in and smacks a big kiss on my lips. "You're freaking amazing." He heads in the direction of the kitchen, a bit more pep in his step than before, and I go back outside to greet the men delivering the dumpsters. There are three large ones in total, but the problem is they're going to have to be dropped off on the other side of the drawbridge and wheeled across so we can use them.

Harlow asked us to work on the sex room while there were no people in the house to see us coming and going from there, so that's our job today. Preferably, I'd like to stick the dumpster under the balcony and just heave everything over the edge, but I'm not sure if we're going to be able to wheel it around there. I need to do a lap around the house to see if there's room. Otherwise, it will sit at the bottom of the portico stairs, and we'll have to carry things in and out.

Luckily, the delivery driver is quick, and we soon have them off the truck and placed on the side of the house. I thank him, and when he leaves, I push one of them back across the drawbridge with me as I go.

Does the drawbridge actually lift up? There are big heavy chains leading to somewhere within the walls, though I have no idea if they're decorative or a functioning mechanism. If they're the latter, we might have to get a mechanic to have a look at them before we try to use them. I'm sure Emma knows someone who could help out with that.

I make my way around to the right side of the house to see if pushing the dumpster under the balcony of the turret is practical. But I can already see the garden is way too overgrown and uneven for me to even attempt it, so I head back around to the front.

Taking the steps two at a time, I throw open both of the entry doors and look between the gap and the dumpster, trying to judge whether the space is wide enough for the dumpster to go through. I'm almost fairly sure it will fit.

"Oli!" I shout, and it echoes through the foyer before I hear his returning shout and the sound of footsteps through the silent house.

"What's up?" he asks, coming to stand by my side.

"Help me push that up the steps. I think we can put it in the foyer so we can just throw things over the balcony once we bring them down in the elevator. It will save us from having to go up and down too many times."

"Yeah, that's a good idea." He smacks me on the ass and skips off toward the bin. Shaking my head at his antics, I follow closely behind him. I hide the smirk that wants to come out thanks to his awkward gait. He needs to stop betting with Harlow, especially with tattoos as the currency. She really is brutal with the placement of them.

Together, with a little bit of muscle and a lot of grunting, we're able to get it up the steps and across the foyer to sit just below the balcony to the side of the staircase. It's not exactly what I had hoped for, but it's better than nothing.

"Close the doors. I worked out how to use the coffee machine, so let's grab a mug before we go upstairs," Oliver suggests, and I'm quick to agree. Although I didn't indulge too much at the gala, it was still a late night, and I really could do with the caffeine kick.

Just as I'm closing the door, a pick-up truck comes down the driveway. Frowning, I close half of the door but leave the other side open behind me and walk to see who it is.

We really need to make adding a driveway a priority. As I walk across the bridge, I recognize the oldest McCallister brother, Miles.

He hops out of the pick-up, looking a little surprised to see me. "Oh hey, Holden. I wasn't expecting anyone to be here." He holds out a hand, and I take it, giving it a quick shake before deciding I'm going to put away any preconceived notions and be friendly. Whatever happened between them and Hope is none of my business. As long as they don't hurt her any more, I can play nicely. Especially because Harlow has her heart set on them fixing up her zoo, not to mention a little matchmaking scheme going on as well.

"Oliver and I thought we'd get a start on clearing out some of the rooms so that Harlow and Jacinta won't have as much work when they get back," I explain.

"Yeah, that was kind of my thinking, too. I wanted to do another walkthrough so I could draw up a few more plans, and I didn't think anyone would be here for me to bother," he tells me apologetically with a sheepish look on his face. "I should have called ahead."

"No, man, that's fine. You're not going to be in our way. You know how to get out the back. Just go around the house, walk over the dry lake, and cross the bridge." He points his keys at the truck and locks it before we start to make our way back over the drawbridge.

"That's not going to be practical once that lake fills in again. I'm assuming that's the plan?" he asks, and I nod.

"Yeah, we're going to run a road down that boundary over there." I point to the left of the property where there looks to be an overgrown dirt access road. The moat and lake stop a few yards before it, and it's wide enough for two vehicles to pass safely.

"That will make things a lot easier. I've got some equipment coming in over the next couple of days. I'll use one of the loaders to clear the track to make it easier for everyone to access right now. That way they won't have to stop at the house to be directed. We'll get some signs made so that everything is easy to see, then people will have no reason to be knocking on your door."

"Thanks, man. I really appreciate it. We talked about it last night, and we decided that it would be best if you guys made all decisions regarding the zoo and who needs to be contracted and whatever. That way we're not double booking or anything. So, if you could get some quotes on having the road surveyed and surfaced, I'd appreciate it."

"Yeah. No problem. I'm happy to take care of that for you. Are you guys going to be moving in here?" He gestures to the house as we stop at the entrance steps.

"Yeah, we are. As soon as Harlow and Jax get back from their cruise, we're going to start moving in. The furniture will probably be donated or sold, but the closets are still filled with clothes, and cupboards need going through, and so many things really." I sigh at the thought of the job ahead of us.

"You guys really have your work cut out for you. Two massive projects going on at the same time."

I slap him on the shoulder, chuckling ruefully. "Which is why I'm *very* glad you guys are taking over the outside part of it. Do you want a coffee?" I offer, but he shakes his head.

"Thanks, but no. I'll just do the walkthrough and make a few more notes. I had some ideas last night."

"Ok, just remember the herd of deer haven't been rounded up yet. Harlow said she and Chuck are going to do it when she gets back. They've got some quarter horses who are trained for cutting, and they said it would be fun."

"Yeah, I've got a fencing contractor coming in to do a deer-safe perimeter around one of the very back paddocks that has a small section of forest as well as some open grazing land in it. I thought that would be perfect for them. He said it should only take a day or two if he brings enough crew." Although he looks pleased by the prospect, there's definitely some skepticism there. Poor guy isn't used to what kind of doors and possibilities open when you're attached to the Summers name.

"It's amazing what you can get done with enough money, isn't it?"

His eyes widen. "You're not wrong. When your dad gave me the budget for the job, I just about fell off my chair, but then again, you guys travel to work in a helicopter, so I guess I shouldn't have been too surprised." He doesn't sound bitter or anything like a lot of people do when they're talking about what we do with our money. That's certainly a plus for him. With Dad making Hope part of our family, she's suddenly become a more than lucrative partner for anyone she chooses to date. "But I've also come to realize how hard you all work, too."

"Oh, speaking of helicopter..." I turn and point to the front of the property. "We're going to need a section of that cleared so a helicopter can land. When you contract a company to do the landscaping, can you mention that to them?"

He takes out his phone and makes a couple of notes. "Yeah, sure. That big section over there should work." He points to the same place I had been thinking. "But we may have to clear a couple more trees away, there and there." I wince slightly when I see where he's gesturing. One of them is a weeping willow, and I know how much Harlow loves them. At least there are a few more on the property, so hopefully she won't be too upset.

"Okay, if that needs to happen, then it needs to happen. I'll leave you to it. Have you got all our contacts in case you can't get hold of Harlow?"

He chuckles, putting his phone back in his pocket. "Grace made sure that I did last night. I now have Harlow, all of your siblings, your dad, Grace, and Howard's numbers."

"Okay, great. Listen, I'm going to give you Hope's too because if you can't get one of us, then she will be the next best option." Do I really need to do this? No. Honestly, I want to test the waters because she's my best friend. I just want her to be happy.

He flinches when I say her name and won't meet my eye. "I already have it," he grinds out. "I had to deal with her when we were having the new logo designed." I can see by his reaction he's not as unaffected by Hope as he pretends.

Hmm, I wonder how that went, especially considering his phrasing doesn't go unnoticed. She hasn't mentioned anything to me, so I'll have to do some digging. It's not like her to not tell me everything.

"Okay, good. She's moving into Dad's house in the next day or two, so you should be able to find her at home if you can't get one of us."

This gets his attention, and his head swings to look at me."She's moving into your dad's place?"

"Well, yes, Dad adopted her. She's a Summers now. Where else would she live?"

"She's a grown ass adult too, so it wouldn't be strange for her to stay in her own place," he snaps, but his face pales as if he just realized what he said and who he said it to. "Shit, sorry."

"We're a close-knit family. We like to be in one another's pockets. If it gets to be too much for you, just let us know, and I'll talk to Dad about finding you somewhere else to live. I know Nana didn't really give you an option."

He sighs heavily. "We'll be at the B&B for a little longer since we paid up for a month before Grace offered us room. That will hopefully give us some time to get used to the idea. I know you know that we have a somewhat shaky history with Hope, but I don't want to cause any problems between you."

"That's between the five of you, and as long as you don't go out of your way to hurt her now, I won't get involved. However, you *do* have to face the reality that she's now a formal part of the family that you've agreed to tie yourselves to. Have you thought about having an open conversation between the five of you? It might go a long way in making your lives a little less tense."

He sighs and shakes his head. "I'm not sure it will make a difference, to be honest. Anyway, I better let you get back to work. I'll catch up with you later." With a wave, he heads off around the house, not giving me a chance to respond.

"Well, okay then. I guess he doesn't want to talk about it," I mutter to myself.

Chapter Four

Oliver

I thought Holden would be right behind me, but he still hasn't come back by the time I pour our coffee. Leaving both mugs on the kitchen counter, I decide to poke around a little. This kitchen is industrial-sized, big enough to run a restaurant out of, but it was probably needed given how much the count entertained. There's a large walk-in pantry that stretches back far enough to get lost, with a couple of rows of shelves that are holding lots of empty labeled containers. The trust must have had it cleaned out once the count had been declared missing. If we're going to move in, we're going to have to do a big grocery order. Maybe I should start a list of things we need. The rest of them are very good at eating the food Mrs.

Heyton makes, but they likely won't think about keeping stock of supplies.

Grabbing my phone out of my pocket, I make note of the labels, but I doubt I've even touched the surface. I think we're eventually going to need a housekeeper like Mrs. Heyton. This house is so big despite seven of us living here, and our schedules will be all over the place. We won't need a whole slew of staff, but we've grown up with the ease of having at least one person to take care of those things. It's not like we're incapable of it, but it's definitely not the first thing that'll be on our minds. Not to mention a baby will be joining our lives and routine in a few months. Consistency will benefit her and us as we sort out how to be parents.

Stepping back out of the pantry, I move to the walk-in fridge and use a big pot to prop the door open. I don't want to get locked inside; god knows Holden would never let me live that down.

Once I'm sure the pot will hold, I start poking around. I think Emma said there was another door further back that leads to a freezer. I need an idea about how much space we have before I start ordering groceries... And, okay, I might also be pretty curious.

Sure enough, at the back of the fridge, there's another door with a handle. A wave of stale air hits me in the face, making me cough a little, when I push it down and step inside. I guess there was no need for the cleaning service to come in and do anything since it was emptied out. I decide to keep playing 'better safe than sorry' by propping a canister in the doorway before I move further into the space.

Like the fridge, it isn't cold, and it's empty except for some shelves and hooks for hanging cuts of meat. I'm just about to turn and head back out when a little flashing light catches my eye. Walking to the back wall, I bend down and move aside the little shelf that's in front of it. There's another keypad like the others that have been placed around the house. If this freezer was full and this shelf had things on it, no one would have noticed it at all.

A little thrill of excitement runs through me as I consider that I may have discovered something new. Emma never mentioned this during her tour, so there's a decent chance that she has no idea it exists. Running my hand across the wall, I can't even feel a seam for a door, so maybe there's nothing there. What could the panel be for then?

"Oh hey, there you are," Holden calls, stepping over the canister. "Sorry I took so long. Miles McCallister was arriving as I closed the doors. He's here to have another look through the zoo."

Normally, I would have asked Holden about their interaction, but I'm too interested in what I've found here to care.

"Oh okay," I respond absently, putting in the same code that worked for all the other doors.

It doesn't do anything, so I sit back on my heels,

the feeling of disappointment huge. I thought for sure it would work. But after a minute of moping, there's a low buzz, a click, and then a door pops open from the wall.

"What the fuck?" Holden breathes as I scramble to my feet, then I feel him crowd in close behind me. I go to grab the edge of the door to pull it open, but he stops me.

"Stop, we don't know what's in there," he warns, but I scoff at the spoilsport.

"Seriously? What could be worse than a dead body?" I ask him. He shrugs, but I wait while he goes back to the kitchen. When he returns, he's holding a large butcher's knife.

"Okay." When he tips his head at the door, I pull it open. It's heavy, much like the one down in the vault, and we cautiously step inside once it's open wide enough for the both of us. Again, like the vault, an automatic light comes on, illuminating the inside of the room. However, *unlike* the vault, this room has a more sinister feel to it. It's concrete, with a drain in the bottom and a chair sitting in the middle of the space. There are shackles on each of the arms and legs, which is definitely not a welcoming sight. On the wall is a cabinet, and I can see a whole heap of tools lying haphazardly on the top. A queasy feeling rolls through my stomach.

"Are those bloodstains?" I ask Holden, pointing to the brown splotches on the floor. He pushes past me and squats down for a closer look.

"Yeah, I think so. Looks like the count added to his depravity with a little bit of torture on the side." He gets up and walks over to have a look at the tools on the counter. After a minute, he frowns and gestures at one of them. "This is weird. All the tools are clean except this one. Why would he have cleaned all the others but left this one?"

Unable to stand not looking, I leave the doorway, solid in the notion that the door is too heavy to slam shut on its own, and hurry over to look at what he's pointing at. One of the knives has a brown patch of dried blood on it, but that's not the only thing that makes it stand out. All the other tools are lined up neatly, like someone took great care in keeping the area tidy, but the dirty knife is lying on the side like someone carelessly tossed it down when they were finished with it.

"Who knows, but this is creepy as fuck. Let's get out of here." A shudder rolls down my skin, but when I turn to leave, Holden moves to the back of the room. I don't really want to follow him, but what other choice do I have? I didn't get my boyfriend back just to lose him to some angry ghosts or whatever the fuck is lying in wait around here. Unsurprisingly, there's yet another door. This one has no panel on it, so he simply pushes the handle, and it opens up to a set of stairs.

"Wow, I'm pretty sure this wasn't on the map, but what's the bet that it leads into the underground tunnel system?" His quiet voice seems to carry through the doorway and down the stairs.

"No bet." I push him out of the way and slam the door shut. "I don't like the fact that this wasn't locked. It means that if you can get into the right tunnel, you can get into this room."

"Yeah, but without the code, you couldn't get past that door." Despite his argument, I drag him with me out of the torture room before pushing the door closed.

"True, but I still don't like it. Dude was fucked up. Thank god the twins weren't raised around him. At least Dad and Nana insist that their dad was nothing like him, which I guess is something to be grateful for." I bend down and pick up the canister, placing it back on the shelf and letting the freezer door close behind us before doing the same thing to the pot when we finally get back to the kitchen. "For now, I don't even want to think about that room. We'll deal with it later. Now, I just want my coffee and to go deal with the secret sex room."

A small smile pulls at Holden's lush lips as I hand him his coffee before we leave the kitchen. "That has nothing to do with wanting to restock it with our own stuff, does it?" he teases, and I shrug, not embarrassed at all.

"Why not? The sex room looks fun, and why shouldn't I want to make use of it with my lovers?" I crowd him up against the wall just next to the painting of the count that opens up to the elevator. Holding my coffee off to the side so I don't spill it on him, I lean in and take his lips, pressing my chest against his.

He kisses me back with a kind of desperation that has been present since we got back together—like he's trying to make up for all the lost time. I don't know how I can soothe that need in him, and even though I want him to feel secure and comfortable in this second chance at our relationship, I'm certainly not complaining about his current enthusiasm. When I pull away, he's breathless and panting, and I can feel how hard his cock is as I rub against it.

But then I recoil with a groan as I brush my new tattoo against it. He chuckles when he looks down and sees me trying to pull my jeans away. "Maybe tight jeans on your new tattoo wasn't such a great idea."

"I didn't think about it when I packed them. I had planned to change when we went past Dad's, but I forgot in our hurry to get here. I might take them off while we're cleaning so it doesn't keep rubbing. Come on." I grab his free hand and drag him up the next flight of stairs to the other secret elevator.

God, I can't believe we're making this our new home. I mean, with the money we have from the family businesses, we've lived a very privileged life with Dad, Nana, and Poppy, but there's something that's special and exciting about our new home. It has something that our family home never had.

I love all the mysteries in the house, and we haven't even started exploring the secret passages between the rooms. Though I'm firmly choosing a 'pretend it doesn't exist' approach with the hidden freezer room. I'll let everyone know what we found at our first family meeting when Harlow and the others get back from the cruise. And by family meeting, I mean Harlow and the rest of the guys. It's one of the ways we're going to attempt to keep this unconventional relationship on track. Because things aren't going to settle down for a while. Not until the renovations on both the house and the zoo are done, and who knows how long that will take. We're heading into winter, and although California weather is mild compared to other parts of the country, there are still going to be delays due to weather.

Plus, my mind reminds me, *there's going to be a baby in all of your lives sooner or later.* Instead of that thought making me panic, it just builds up the warm fuzzies that I have when I think of Harlow and Holden. The baby isn't any of ours, not biologically, anyway, but it will be another little puzzle piece to complete the family we're building.

"Are you as excited about all of this as I am?" I ask my boyfriend as he programs the code into the elevator. "Running Neighpalm Ink is awesome, and opening the new store in New York is exciting, but it's kind of all done now. Staff are hired, and the shop is fitted out. After the grand opening, it's done. I'm kind of getting bored."

He frowns, looking a little worried. "But I thought you loved tattooing. Has that changed?" he questions, and I carefully think about my answer. This whole honesty thing needs to apply to our relationship with Harlow, but it also needs to be an essential part in our relationship with one another, too.

"No, I still love tattooing, but I kind of love building up a business from scratch. What we're doing here is exciting, and I've loved watching how thrilled Harlow has been when she's been talking about her plans for the zoo. It's how I felt when I was building Neighpalm Ink. I love Harlow's idea of taking abandoned places and renovating them. I'm thinking maybe I might start looking at starting a nonprofit housing thing. Buy up old, abandoned places and renovate them into homeless shelters or affordable housing to help people get back on their feet. Or even something for foster kids aging out of the system. A place where they can go when their foster parents don't want them anymore. Somewhere safe to live while they finish their schooling or look for a job and establish themselves as adults. You and I and the others got lucky, *so* freaking lucky, but so many of us don't. And as much as I want to foster and adopt, there are only so many we can take."

He's staring at me now like he doesn't know me and can't believe the words coming out of my mouth, but his eyes are shining with so much love and a heap of pride. "Wow, Oli, I think that's an awesome idea. I had no idea you felt that way, but I am so impressed. I guess it's kind of like how I wanted to take over the day-to-day management of Ninja Starfish. Running Neighpalm Records has been a dream come true, but it's also taken me away from my music, and I miss being involved with bands and touring and all of that kind of thing. I'm ready to hand more of the responsibilities to Hope and the rest of the team and start getting my hands dirty again, so to speak."

This right here makes me so fucking happy. I'm thrilled for Holden to get back into his music. He used to play all the time, but he's so busy organizing all his clients' careers that he hasn't picked up a guitar or sat down at the piano in so long. I know he'll still be taking care of Ninja Starfish, but I'm kind of hoping that he'll be so involved he won't be able to help himself. Music has always been such a big thing for him. Even back in the group home, we would sit for hours, sharing earbuds and listening to playlists he'd made. Our first time together was to one of those playlists. I still can't listen to any of those songs without getting hard. There's a spark back in his eyes that dimmed a long time ago. Our break-up certainly didn't help, but at least back then he still had his music lessons. It was when he took over as CEO and had less and less time to play that it finally dimmed completely. Harlow has certainly been helping it return, and I'm hoping I've had some part in it as well. This career move will only solidify it for him.

"Well, it sounds like both of our lives will be changing in the next coming months," I say to him as the elevator doors open, then we both step into the sex dungeon. "But for now, let's get this room cleaned out. I've already found a supplier to replace all this equipment. The red leather is too gaudy. Plus, Harlow made a comment about Jax's granddaddy defiling women on these, and now I can't get it out of my head."

Holden shudders as he gazes around the room in amazement. This is his first time up here, so I patiently wait as he takes it all in. "And now I have a picture of an old man with wrinkly balls railing into a pretty woman across that bench there."

"That's weirdly specific, man." He shrugs and points at the bed inside the birdcage. "How about we start with stripping all the furniture and ditching all the cushions and things on the bed and in the pit. It's light, and we should be able to pile a lot of it into the elevator with us," he suggests, and I nod, going over to the role playing wardrobe.

"There's a whole heap of costumes and things in here that can join them. Let's keep piling things in until we have no room, then we can move on to the rest of the stuff." I look down at the pit and grimace. "We should have brought gloves."

Holden frowns. "Yeah, maybe we should have. I'll dig around in the wardrobe and see if there's anything in there. Who knows what they might have been used for, but it'd probably be better than nothing."

"Well, I guess that's as good a place as any to start. Did I tell you I found a supplier to replace all of these things, too?" He's too entranced in the wardrobe to hear me.

"Holy shit, the count really was kinky." He runs his hand over one of the furries' heads just like I did. He looks up at me. "You want to try something like this?" Instead of being disgusted, he sounds curious.

"I like to try everything once, and it could be fun," I reply, not meeting his eye. I've barely finished speaking when a finger presses under my chin, lifting my head up until our eyes meet.

"I'm certainly not one to shame anybody for their kinks. We'll have to sit down and do the order together."

And just like that, my embarrassment leaves and my cock hardens. I shift because it's not comfortable in my jeans, and he looks down at it.

"I'd take care of that, but there isn't a surface I feel comfortable doing you on at the moment. Let's have a rain check until we can find one we know for sure is clean."

My turn to wrinkle my nose as I lean in and kiss him. "Agreed, but I *am* going to take my jeans off to give my tattoo some breathing space."

"Okay, make sure they don't get mixed up with everything," he tells me as he starts to pull costumes off hangers and pile them in his arms.

"Ha, could you imagine that? What would Nana say if I came home with no pants on?" I laugh as I undo my jeans and slide them down my legs. Going back out, I look for somewhere to put them and end up draping them over a paddling bench. Holden follows me out and pushes the button on the elevator.

"Okay, let's do this. I can't wait until Harlow comes home and sees what we've done."

Chapter Five

Harlow

My head pounds and my stomach rolls with nausea as I try to force my eyes open, a small groan tumbling out of my mouth. God, did I drink too much last night? I try to move, but I can't make my limbs cooperate, and as my mind starts to unfuzz, I realize a few things that have my heart racing. I'm not on a bed, and the reason I can't move my limbs is because they're tied down.

My eyes snap open, and I can see I'm tied to a chair. What the fuck? Moving my head slowly because it's pounding, I look around where I'm being kept. It appears to be a basement, but there's only a dim light from the stairway, so I can't really make anything else out.

A small sound has me moving my head in the

opposite direction. There, tied to chairs just like me, are Jaxon and Jacinta.

Fuck. I remember now. We were in the limo on the way to the cruise ship. Smoke started filling the cabin. Those eyes in the mirror. I swear I recognized them, but now I'm not so sure. Maybe it was my mind playing tricks on me.

Jacinta groans again, so I know she's okay, but when I look at Jax, a small sob comes out. I can just manage to make out his features. His face is bruised and swollen like he's been beaten. What happened? Who would have done that? Then a cold chill runs through me, and I shiver, unable to stop myself. *The stalker.* My head swings around despite the fogginess, and I squint, trying to take in our surroundings. It definitely looks like a basement. There's a small hanging bulb that lets off a dull light. I can see a window, but it's so caked with dirt and dust that it's basically useless. There's a door on the other side of the room and a set of stairs leading upward. Apart from us and the chairs we're tied to, there's nothing else down here.

"Harlow, what's going on?" Jacinta loudly whispers at me. "Where are we?" I struggle to get myself out of my restraints, but I'm having absolutely no luck. Whoever tied me up knew what they were doing.

"I don't know, but I'm guessing my stalker finally had some luck." When I look up at her, her eyes are wide with panic. Her breath is coming out way too fast. She starts to struggle too, but neither of us can get our restraints to move.

"Fuck." I slump back in my chair to think things through. Before I can come up with anything, I hear a door open. The stairs creak ominously as someone starts to descend—make that two some-ones as it's two sets of feet that slowly walk down the steps, the tension in the room ratcheting up as we wait to see who appears.

"You fucking cunt," Jacinta snarls when the first person comes into our line of sight. Cecelia has a smug grin on her face, and when she reaches the bottom of the steps, she moves to the side, giving us eyes on the other person. She's familiar. I can't quite put a name to a face, but it turns out Jacinta sure can.

"Raquel, I always knew you were stupid, but this just proves it. You're already in enough trouble thanks to trying to sell company secrets. They'll throw the book at you for this, and you'll be in jail just like that crazy bitch that's obsessed with Thomas." Oh, this is Jaxon's fired PA. I remember her now. His ex who didn't take their break-up well.

Raquel looks confused at the mention of Veron-ica, but she quickly shakes it off when she catches sight of broken and beaten Jaxon. Then she loudly cries out and runs over to him.

"What did you do?" she demands of Cecelia, but the bitch continues to smirk.

"He started to wake up before we were ready, so he was knocked out."

"Oh, my poor love," Raquel coos as she runs a gentle hand over his face while Cecelia rolls her eyes.

"What do you want with us?" I ask her calmly, not giving her the reaction she wants if her frown is anything to go by.

"To be honest, I don't want *you* at all. I don't think you're necessary to this plan. It's the twins we needed, only one of them, really. You've fucked everything up for us, but the boss insisted we still needed you."

I frown, trying to process everything that she said.

"I need to pee," Jacinta demands, and Cecelia snorts with disgust. She pulls out a gun from the back of her pants and points it at Jaxon.

"Raquel, quit fawning over that idiot, so you can untie Jacinta." She turns her focus to my sister. "As for you, if you even so much as breathe wrong, I'll kill your brother."

Raquel bites her lip and looks between Jaxon and Jacinta. "But you promised me I could have him!" she whines, but Cecelia just gestures with the gun.

"Hurry up, or I'll put a bullet in you just like we did Luke when he became a problem. We don't need you."

"Mom and Dad won't let you kill me! You're

such a fucking bitch." Holy shit. Are these two sisters? Now that I look at them closely, I can see a slight family resemblance. There's just enough to believe it now that I'm seeing them in the same place at the same time. How did that get missed in the background checks? They must have applied under different names, so no one ever connected it. They must have some excellent fake documents.

"Dad is whipped and will do whatever Mom tells him to. Just help the spoiled bitch to the bathroom and try not to let her kick your ass, or I will shoot him *and* you." Stepping closer to Jaxon, she holds the gun against his forehead. Jacinta whimpers, the sound small and desperate, and Cecelia gets this ugly smile on her face that I've never seen before.

I watch as Raquel helps Jacinta to her feet and walks her over to the closed door. Pushing it open, she shuffles Jacinta in, following after her, and I can hear Jacinta say, "Are you really going to stand there and watch? Could you at least turn around?"

I don't hear Raquel's response, but they return soon after the toilet flushes. When they do, Raquel shoves Jacinta into her chair, ties her back up, and steps back.

Cecelia lowers the gun she had pointed at Jaxon. "See, if you cooperate, everyone is going to be okay," she assures me, but I can tell she's lying. There's a glint in her eyes that promises she'd be distinctly unhappy if everyone was okay at the end of this. There's no way they'll leave us alive after this. Not only do we know who they are, but we now know that there's a family connection between them and even more people involved. We're three loose ends. When I look at Jacinta, I can tell that she realizes this too. A tear trickles down her cheek since she's unable to stop it with her hands bound.

"Look, if it's money you want, just tell me how much. Dad will cut you a check," I tell her. "Or one of the businesses? I'm sure he would gladly sign one over to you if you let us go." I wasn't holding up high hopes that she'd negotiate that, and my hopelessness is confirmed when she laughs.

"Oh, Harlow, nice try. What we want is far more valuable than anything your dad could offer us. What we're after will set us up for life," Cecelia gloats while Raquel paws at Jaxon again. She's climbed onto his lap and is busy placing little kisses over his bruises and cooing to him. Gritting my teeth and clenching my fists, I try not to let it bother me that she's writhing on my unconscious boyfriend's lap. Jacinta, of course, isn't so patient.

"Get off my brother, you whore. He's a taken man, practically married. He doesn't want anything to do with *you*."

With a snarl, Raquel climbs off his lap and stomps over to Jacinta, delivering a backhand that snaps her head to the side. Jacinta grunts at the impact, and a trickle of blood appears where her lip has split.

"Who are you calling a whore? Wouldn't that be the woman who's fucking six men at once?" She points at me, and I chuckle.

"Well, I haven't had all six at once. I'm not sure if that's on the table, to be honest," I tell her, trying to get her away from Jacinta. They already said they need just one of the twins. I don't want to push them closer to deciding they'll get rid of the troublesome one to make their lives easier. "But I'm happy to give it a go. Jaxon probably would be, too. He's a virile man, such a high sex drive. I'm usually exhausted after he's finished fucking me."

I try to hit her trigger points, and sure enough, she screeches and lunges at me. This time, it's my head snapping back. It hurts like a bitch, but I'm not willing to let her see how much. When we make it out of this—if we make it out of this—I can let myself feel it then.

"You hit like a child. Is that all you've got? Jaxon did more damage fucking my mouth than you just did." She lunges at me again, and as she hits me, my chair tumbles backward. I can't hold back a startled shriek when I hit the floor, my tied arms trapped against the ground. She starts pulling at my hair and scratching my face.

"For fuck's sake!" Cecelia shouts, trying to pull her sister off of me. "Get your shit together. We can't kill her yet. Do you want us to lose our leverage?"

Raquel spits on me and walks away, wiping her

mouth on the back of her hand. Thankfully, she has shitty aim, so it lands on my chest, with my shirt protecting me from the worst of it.

"Stop riling my sister up, or I'll let her beat the shit out of you. Our leverage needs to be breathing, but a little blood won't take away your value," Cecelia warns while she rights my chair. As she walks away and pulls Raquel into a corner where they whisper fight with one another, I wiggle my arms in the hope that I haven't broken anything in the fall. I stop suddenly when the back of my chair wobbles ever so slightly. It must have been damaged when we landed so hard on it. Hopefully, they won't notice. My mind races with possibilities. If I can get them to leave, we might have a chance to get out of here. I rack my brain for how I can do that, but I've got nothing. Without knowing what they want, I have no clue how I can manipulate them.

A small movement to my side has me turning away from the arguing sisters and looking at my boyfriend. Unlike Jacinta and me, he hasn't got his arms tied behind the back of his chair. His chair has shackles that have been fastened around his wrists, and my heart starts to race when I see one of his hands opening and closing. Looking up, I just about sob when his beautiful yet swollen aquamarine eyes meet mine.

"Oh, thank god," I whisper quietly enough for only Jacinta to hear. She sighs in relief, her split lip having stopped bleeding. "Are you okay? What happened?"

He blinks a couple of times while his eyes scan the room to get his bearings. They almost bug out of his head when he catches sight of Raquel. But I can see him thinking quickly, and when he turns to me, there's an apology in his eyes.

"I'm sorry. Don't believe a word that's about to come out of my mouth," he whispers. What is he talking about?

"Raquel, baby! What are you doing here? I missed you so much!" Jaxon pitches his voice like he's hurting, and I can see the minute she hears him.

Cecelia tries to hold her sister back, but she shakes her off and rushes over to Jaxon.

"Do you mean that? *Really* mean it?" she asks as she pushes his hair back off his face in a gentle manner.

"You don't know how much. I was an idiot to let you go. Do you know what my asshole brothers wanted? They wanted us to share a woman! I went along with it because I didnt want to cause any problems, but why the fuck would I want to share a woman when I could have you all to myself? I was going to break it off with Harlow on the cruise, then come find you when we returned," he tells her. Her eyes slide to me, a triumphant smile on her face.

I know he said not to believe what he said, but

unfortunately, he hit the hot button that has been my biggest worry the whole time, so the hurt on my face is real. Raquel looks thrilled to see it there.

"What the fuck? Are you kidding me?" Jacinta yells at him, not having heard what he whispered to me. On the downside, my eardrums might be permanently damaged, but on the bright side, it will help sell the whole charade.

"Let me out of here, so we can be together," he encourages her, and she spins around, holding out her hand to her sister.

"Give me the keys. I'll make him take me away, and you'll still have one of the twins for the blood you need."

Of course, they need the twins' blood for the vault. But the drugs and guns are gone. What else could they want?

Cecelia snorts and rolls her eyes. "Yeah, that's not going to happen, you stupid bitch. He's playing you."

Raquel snarls, and her fists clench tightly as she takes a step toward her sister, I cross my fingers that she will attack Cecelia.

"What is your fucking problem? Why should you be the one in charge? You fucked up as much as I did! You couldn't let go of your resentment for Harlow and screwed it all up. If you had played nicely, you would still be firmly established in Neighpalm Industries. Instead, we had to resort to kidnapping."

Why would Cecelia resent me?

Cecelia grunts with annoyance. "Like you can fucking talk. If you hadn't fucked up with Jaxon, we'd be even closer to getting what we want. You'd have full access to that house and could find what we need."

"You *both* fucked up. You're lucky you're not dead like Luke is," a harsh voice says from the stairway, and the girls exchange a panicked look. We hadn't noticed anyone on the stairs because we were too engrossed with their argument, but their heavy footsteps have Cecelia and Raquel practically ready to run. The visitor is inspiring a completely different reaction in me. Who is he?

There's something about that voice that's hitting me as familiar, but I can't figure out why. Squinting through the dark, I try to make out who it is; with the distance, no features are distinguishable yet. "And if you don't shut up, I have two bullets with your names on them. I can easily put them between your eyes," he threatens as he steps off the stairs and into the dull light. My stomach rolls when I recognize the man. How could this be happening? I don't understand how I could be such a bad judge of character.

An evil grin gives his face a sinister twist as he turns to look at me. "Hello, Harlow, it's been a while."

Chapter Six

Holden

I'm a dusty mess once lunchtime swings around. We ended up deciding to start in the safe room, removing all the clothing and linens and everything from there. Turns out the mattress on the huge bed was separate pieces, so it was quite easy for me and Oli to grab them one at a time and bring them up the spiral staircase. Thank goodness it was wide, or navigating those curves would have been a problem. Not that we didn't come across some surprises anyway. Oli's scream when a baby mouse ran across his arm was hysterical, and it took me a couple of minutes to stop laughing while he pouted the whole time.

The bed frame itself is in perfect condition, but it could probably do with a sanding and a new stain to keep it that way. It will have to be a job for one of us because we don't want to let any workmen up into this room. Kai likes to do things with his hands, so he's probably the best option.

It took us numerous trips up the stairs with all the clothes and shoes the count had in his wardrobe. He had some jewelry and watches, but we left them for Jaxon to have a look at. They were classic pieces, and it might be nice for him to have something from his grandfather despite how depraved he may have been. All that's left in there now are empty hangers and the contents of the safe that we left intact.

"I think that's it for down here," Oli says after looking around the room. "Shall we head upstairs and start dealing with the sex stuff?" He waggles his eyebrows at me, and my dick pulses in my shorts. Both of us were too tired last night once the gala was over, so we just collapsed into bed and snuggled. But he's been parading around in his tight boxers, as well as stripping off his shirt when he started to itch from the dust, and my self-control only goes so far. At this stage, I don't care that the equipment is used. I'm sure twenty-five years of non-use has made them practically sterile again.

He must see the lust in my eyes because a wicked little grin appears on his face before he turns and sprints up the stairs. I follow quickly after him. As fun as it has been being submissive to Harlow, it's been a while since I let my dominant side out, and there are so many lovely things to play with that I'm going to take full advantage of them.

When we took a quick break earlier, I had a closer look at all the equipment in the room. There are a couple of paddling benches, stocks, a padded wall with restraints, two chairs for strapping people down, and a St. Andrew's Cross, but the one thing that really caught my eye looks like a cross between one of Oli's tattoo tables and a doctor's exam chair. It's a waist-high horse with arm, leg, and head rests that have built-in restraints. The headrest is one of those ones that you can put your face into and see out the other side like a massage table. I found a bottle of disinfectant under the sink in the bathroom and gave it a good spray and wipe while Oli was exploring the rest of the room.

Oli is hiding behind one of the crosses when I get to the top of the stairs, and I snort. "Babe, that's never going to hide you."

He peeks out from behind it and winks. "I guess you need to punish me for my bad hide-and-seek skills."

My dick throbs again, and a grin curls my lips. "Oh, babe, that's *exactly* what I have planned."

I stride toward him, and he doesn't bother to run. Pulling him to me, he leans in for a kiss, but I spin him so the arm I had a hold of is now behind him while his back presses to my front. I lean in and bite his neck, savoring the groan he gives me in response. "Kissing is for pets that deserve a reward, and you haven't been a good boy yet." I run my tongue over the shell of his ear as I whisper those words, smiling when goosebumps rise all over his flesh. Oli has always been deliciously responsive.

With his arm behind his back, I march him over to the piece of furniture that I'm most interested in. He balks slightly, but I nip at his ear to deliver a little sting. "I wiped over everything."

His head turns to look at me, his pretty brown eyes widening in surprise. "When did you get time to do that?" he asks. I push in the center of his back, and he immediately obeys, leaning onto the apparatus.

"When you were downstairs and more interested in the count's shoes than anything else. You got distracted for about ten minutes, and I made use of the time wisely," I reassure him as I strap his arms into the arm rests, followed by his head. I slide his boxer briefs over his perky ass cheeks and down his legs before he steps out of them. Throwing them to the side, I help him put his legs on the leg rests before I strap those in too. Then I step back and admire how my boyfriend looks, all bound and tied for me. I run my hand over his ass cheeks, which are so nicely displayed and parted from how he's strapped in. "Oh, babe, if only Harlow could see you now." I lean in to run my tongue over his puckered ass hole, and he squirms. He tastes salty and musky, and I hold my dick through my clothes as I feel pre-cum soak my underwear.

His breathing is already becoming heavy, and when I reach underneath his body, his cock is hard and pulsing. I step back and strip off my clothes and toss them to the side. Palming my dick once more, my hand lazily slides up and down as I take in his sexy form laid out for my enjoyment.

"Please," he begs, so I come closer and adjust the leg restraints until I can slip into the space between his legs. I rest my body over his, getting in nice and close to his ear again, thrilled by the heat of his body against my skin.

"Please what?" I ask, and he pants.

"Please, anything. Touch me, or let me touch you."

"Not just yet. I think I'll have a look in the toy cupboard." Stepping away from him, I leave him waiting while I move over to the cabinet. I noticed there was a whole heap of still packaged toys. Pulling open the doors, I check out what's on offer. My eyebrows jump when I take note of the packaging. It's an older style, one that must be from when I wasn't old enough to know about sex toys, but it's definitely Sugar and Spice labeling. Aunt Merideth's company has been around for a long time.

Next, I search for a bottle of lube. Grabbing both things, I tear the wrapping off the plug and drizzle some of the lube over it before returning to Oli.

I dribble a generous amount of lube over his puckered hole, and I feel him shudder at the cool intrusion. Using my fingers, I work some into the tight ring, and he groans before the pleading starts again.

"Please."

I give him a sharp slap on the ass. "Be patient and quiet, or I will gag you," I threaten even though I plan on gagging him with my dick after I'm done here. Once I'm happy with how much lube he has and I've worked his hole, my hand slips around to his balls, grabbing hold of them as I work the plug into his ass. Back and forth, I watch his tight ring stretch around the intrusion. It's not huge, but it's big enough that it takes a while for me to work it in. Eventually, it gets past the tight ring of muscle and slides forward, settling between his parted cheeks. I've been holding Oli's balls tightly, and he's been moaning the entire time.

"Oh, Oli, that wasn't quite like I instructed. I think you need to be punished." My Dom side is new to Oli. I only discovered it once we had broken up; I had decided to explore my sexuality a little more when I got older. This is really the first time he's seeing it as my partner. I hadn't wanted to scare him away when we were just working through our feelings for one another again, but I should have known better. My boyfriend is a kinky fuck. I let go of his balls and lightly run my finger down his pierced dick, the little bars in it cold to the touch. I lightly tug on one, and I revel in the way his body jumps.

Leaving him there, I go back to the cupboard and grab a dark red and black flogger. The way Oli's ass cheeks bounced in front of me as he walked up and down the stairs really inspired me, and I want to see what they look like, all red and covered in my marks.

Unwrapping it, I leave the wrapping in the cupboard and go back to him. His head is strapped into the headrest, so I walk around to the front of him, my erect dick in line with his mouth, though I stand far enough away that he can't reach it. He whines in disappointment, and I crouch down so I can see his face. "I know we haven't talked much about this, but I need to know you're okay with what I'm about to do." I show him the flogger, and although he swallows nervously, he has love and trust in his eyes.

"I trust you, babe," he says, his voice a little husky, so I lean in to place a soft kiss on his lips.

"Thank you," I whisper, but when I pull away, I reassume my Dom persona. "I need your safe word, Oliver," I say to him, and he shudders as I walk around his body, lightly dragging the end of the flogger along his skin to build anticipation. He's quiet for a moment while he's thinking about it.

"Corncob," he tells me, and I stop what I'm doing.

"Seriously?" I ask him, and he shrugs as best he can in spite of the restraints.

"Yeah. It's not like I'll shout that out while we're having sex."

"Okay then, but only use it if you mean it." I run my hands over his delicious buttcheeks and down his thighs.

The trick to flogging is hitting the meaty parts of his thighs so that it doesn't hurt as much as hitting bone that's close to the surface. So you want to avoid the spine and just get the sections on either side of it. Unless your aim is to cause pain, then have at it, but I don't like hardcore pain. I like to make it hurt just enough to get the blood flowing and build an endorphin response in my subs.

Stepping back enough, I line up so that I'm going to hit him across his thighs with more than just the tips. The tips hurt more, and I want to build him up as I'm pretty sure this is his first time. So I want to be gentler to start. I want him to want to do this with me often, not hate it.

"Oli, I'm going to give you three lashes on each side. Be a good boy and keep quiet, and you will be rewarded." I nudge the plug in his ass with the handle of the flogger, and he remains quiet aside from a grunt that slips out.

"Good boy," I praise him before raising my hand. With gentle, even strokes, I lash him in a figure-eight motion—first the left side, then the right. One, two, three, four, five, and six. The last two cause him to groan, and I smile. I know his pain threshold is high because of his love of tattoos, but hearing that is music to my ears; it means I can punish him some more.

I drop the flogger and step closer, running my hands over both cheeks. "Oh dear, you weren't quiet like I asked you to be. Which means I have to punish you more." I give him a sharp slap on each cheek before going around to the front of him. I want to see his face to make sure he's not hiding the wrong kind of pain. He has tears in his eyes, which is reason enough to pause for a second and check in.

"Do you want to use your safe word, Oli?" I ask, and he shakes his head as much as he can.

"No, please, I want you to punish me." I smile at his words and step into him.

"Well, since you can't seem to be quiet on your own, how about I make you?" Lining my cock up with his lips, I tap his shoulder.

"Open your mouth so I can fuck your face." He does as I tell him, and I thrust my hips forward, filling his hot wet mouth. I push past his gag reflex until his nose is resting against my pelvis. Holding there, I feel him struggle, but I don't pull out until my dick throbs. His eyes are streaming even more tears as he gasps for breath. I let him recover before I go again.

"Oh yeah, fuck, I can feel your throat closing around me," I groan as it constricts around me before I pull out again. "Again," I order as I thrust back and forth a few times, really fucking his face.

When I pull away, there's saliva dripping from the corner of his lips, and he's panting. Running a gentle hand through his hair, I step back.

"Such a good boy, I think you need a reward now." I move around to the back of him, running my fingers along his spine. "This time, you can make as much noise as you want," I tell him before pulling the plug out of his ass with a sharp yank. He yelps, but I ignore it as I look down, watching his asshole slowly try to close back up. Grabbing the lube, I pour a generous amount over my cock, sliding my hand up and down to mix it with Oli's saliva before lining myself up and plunging into his dark hole. He shouts at the intrusion, and I moan as his tight passage wraps around my dick.

I pull back and slam in again, my orgasm just out of reach from all of the foreplay. Leaning over my lover, I reach around and grab his dick. I thrust in and out of him, loving the feeling of his ass gripping my cock so tightly, the wet slip of lube making it a smooth glide. My hand works his dick, and he grunts as I fuck him hard. My toes curl when my orgasm bursts into me, and I slam my dick deep as I furiously pump his. Oliver shouts, then his dick pulses, his cum shooting all over the floor under him as well as all over my hand.

I slow my hand and bring it up to my mouth, licking it clean. "Such a good boy," I croon before placing little kisses all over his back. He's quiet as he tries to regain control of his breathing, and I'm a little concerned it's too much. My hips and thighs have been slamming into his flogged skin continuously.

"Are you okay, babe?" I ask quietly, and he sighs, my heart sparking in worry.

"I'm awesome," he replies dazedly, and I practically deflate with relief. Pulling out of him, I undo the restraints and leave him floating as I go in search of a cloth to clean up both us and the floor.

My phone rings just as I'm digging around in the bathroom. Hurrying back to my pile of clothes, I bend over and grab it out of my shorts, seeing Declan's name on the screen.

"Hey, man, what's up?" I ask him, standing back up. Oli's naked body presses against mine, and he winds his arms around my waist, leaning his head on my shoulder.

"Where are you two?" he asks, and I smile at my bossy big brother as Oli's hands run over my body.

"We're at the count's place, though we're going to have to start calling it something else," I muse, and Oli lifts his head.

"Our place." My smile spreads even wider. Yeah, I like that—*our place.*

"Well, drop whatever you're doing and get back into the city. We're still at the hotel, and Kai and Thomas need us. We're getting drunk."

I stiffen up, all the languidness from fucking Oli into submission disappearing in a instant.

"What's going on? Why?" I ask, but he's already hung up. I frown at the phone, and when I turn around, Oli is already back in his boxer briefs and looking for his shirt. When he finds it, he scrunches up his face.

"Can we just pop home and grab a change of clothes and a shower? I'm all sweaty and dusty and gross."

"Yeah, but we need to be quick. Declan sounded pissed off," I tell him as I pull my clothes on. "We'll come back and finish this tomorrow."

Oliver, who has put on his jeans and found his shoes and socks, hurries over to the elevator and calls it while I finish dressing.

The two of us can't help talking about it as we climb into the elevator. "I wonder what the problem is. And why the fuck is Thomas still here? I thought he was going with Harlow, Jax, and Jazzy." Oliver can't hide the concern in his voice, and a prick of worry nags at my mind.

"Shit, I don't know, but it must be big if he voluntarily stayed behind." When the elevator gets to the bottom, we step out, and Oli slides the painting of the lady back in front of the doors, concealing it. In a matter of minutes, we're in the car, rushing back to the house, and it's not long before we're off to meet our brothers and find out what the fuck is going on.

We know we've found them when we get to the cocktail lounge, where a sign on the door says *Closed for Private Function.* The two of us exchange a look, and I push open one of the doors. The room looks to be empty, but I can hear murmuring coming from a secluded booth in one of the corners.

Oli and I wind our ways through the other tables. Although smoking is no longer allowed inside bars and restaurants, there's still that scent of stale smoke and beer permeating the room. I wrinkle my nose. "Someone needs to tell Jax that this bar needs an overhaul. Replacing the carpets and curtains should help with the smell."

"Not going to stop people from spilling drinks though," Oli points out as we arrive at the booth filled with three of my brothers.

"About damn time," Declan grumbles, and Oli flips him off.

"My car is fast, but I still wanted to avoid a ticket, thank you very much," he replies testily as he throws himself into the booth, leaving me hovering.

"Grab yourselves a drink before you sit down," Kai suggests, waving his empty glass around. I can tell by the number of glasses on the table that I might need to grab us two or three to catch up.

"Just bring the bottle. No, make it two," Thomas says morosely, staring down into his empty glass.

I look at Declan, who nods subtly. "Grab them, then we'll fill you both in on what's happening."

Kai salutes me with his empty glass. "Don't take too long." He's already on his way to being drunk, which doesn't happen all that often. He likes to say his body is a temple, so he doesn't like to poison it.

Raising my eyebrows, I hurry back to the empty bar. They must have given the staff the day off. I fill an ice bucket with ice and grab two more glasses and two bottles of whiskey, then, with my arms full, I make my way back to the table.

Chapter Seven

Kai

When Holden gets back to the table, I grab the bottle of whiskey from his hand and pour myself another generous glass, not bothering with ice. I listen on morosely, sipping my drink, while Declan and Thomas explain what occurred with Veronica to Oli and Den.

Learning that you're expecting a child should be a joyous occasion; instead, I'm miserable. I had dared to dream that it would one day be Harlow with my baby inside her, but I'm locked in this nightmare where Harlow is replaced by Veronica. Not to mention she insists the baby is my brother's, not mine. As much as I don't want to be having a baby with Veronica, it's a kick in the guts that she won't accept the baby as mine. I'm not good enough for her... just like my father wasn't good enough for my mother.

"What a fucking bitch," Oli bursts out when Declan and Thomas finish, then he turns to me. "I'm sorry this is happening to you. We just need to think of her as an incubator and hope the baby looks like you so we don't have any reminders of her."

I wave him off. "I don't want to talk about it anymore today. Let me wallow in my misery." I look at Thomas. "*Our* misery because he's going to be the one who has to suffer through dealing with her. Tomorrow, I'll get my head on straight and start doing things a dad should be doing."

"Cheers to that." Oli raises his glass, and the rest of my brothers clink theirs against it before drinking. "Cheers to the next generation of Summers. Because as sucky as this is, it's exciting to be welcoming a baby."

"That's true," says Declan, "and I have a couple of ideas I want to run past you guys about future-proofing our family."

"And I want to know what the two of you were doing at the count's today," Thomas says, and Oli vehemently shakes his head.

"You mean *our* place," he says very firmly. I feel a flash of excitement overtake my misery. "We need to start calling it our place."

"Yeah, I like the sound of that," I tell him, sitting up a little straighter. We have a wonderful home with Dad, but this will be something of our own that we can mold and shape into what we want. A blank slate for our family to grow and flourish, giving me some of the control that is so sorely lacking in the situation with Veronica.

"Hang on, before we get into what we were doing, what about you?" Holden asks Thomas. "Did you speak to the others and tell them why you didn't make it before the cruise left?"

Tom frowns, shaking his head. "No, I haven't had a chance to. I'll do that now. I'm sure they've realized that I didn't make it." His pauses, his brow starting to get that little furrow that means he's probably starting to catastrophize something. "Actually, I'm surprised they haven't tried to call me. I'll try Harlow first. I'm sure Jaxon is probably busy." He pulls his phone out, and I watch as he calls our girlfriend.

God, I wish she was here. That I could bury my face in her shoulder as she wraps her arms around me and assures me everything is going to be alright. She's given me a sense of peace that has been missing in my life for so long. Don't get me wrong, my family is amazing, and I wouldn't be the man I am without them, but for so long I felt I had to keep busy to prove I was worth the Summers name. I know I'm guilty of using the adrenaline rush of extreme sports to block out the insidious thoughts that would creep back in if I let myself sit too quietly for too long.

No matter how lucky you are to be placed with a kind and amazing family like the Summers, the scars from my trauma—thanks to my mother's addiction and her resentment of me and my father— never went away. We hadn't been enough for her, so I'm beyond grateful that I've found a woman who accepts me, flaws and all. Harlow wants nothing more than to love me and be loved by me. Although I know this isn't the ideal situation, she was amazing when she found out that I'm the father of Veronica's baby, and I'm sure she'll support us through this whole charade as well.

"Kai, get out of your head," Declan commands royally, and I roll my eyes at him. Just like big brother to assume I'm worrying instead of having the comforting realization that I've got a ride or die woman on my hands.

Tom pulls his phone away from his ear, frowning. "She's got it turned off. It went straight to messages."

"Try Jazzy," Holden suggests as he leans back in the booth, sighing. "She never turns hers off."

We watch as he tries first our sister, then Jaxon, getting the same response each time.

"Maybe their phones don't work out there." Oli leans back against his boyfriend, and I smile. I'm so glad they worked things out. There's always been a strained relationship between the two of them, and it's nice that it's been repaired. I'm just sad it took so long, but maybe that's for the best. If they had stayed together as teenagers, who knows if they would have lasted for the long haul.

"They should," Declan grunts, "but I guess they might have wanted a break without them. If they don't call us by this evening, once they've realized Tom's not there, then I'll call the ship. I'm pretty sure Jaxon said he left the contact details with Dad."

"Alright, enough of this. What were you two doing out at our place so early this morning after the gala?" I point my whiskey glass at my two brothers. Noticing it's empty, I hold it out to be filled. Thomas leans in and obliges, but he puts a couple of cubes of ice in it. Probably a good idea, even if it only waters it down a little bit. I can really feel the alcohol kicking in now.

"We thought we would get a start on clearing out the panic room and sex room before there are too many people coming in and out of the house. The dumpsters were also delivered today, so we were there to meet them."

I perk up at hearing about the sex room. I haven't had a chance to see it yet, only Oli and Holden have, but it sounds fun.

"And did Harlow decide she wanted to keep the sex room, or does she want to get rid of it?" I ask, secretly crossing my fingers for the former. Thomas and Declan both look like they're eager to hear Harlow's response as well, and a small chuckle escapes my mouth. Everyone looks at me, but I wave them away. "Nothing, carry on."

"Oh, she definitely wants to keep it, but she talked about replacing the furniture, and when Oli and I examined it today, it looked like it was in really good condition. It's been really well maintained." Holden keeps going on, but I start to tune him out, more focused on the blush that's staining Oli's cheeks.

"Ha, you guys totally tested it out, didn't you?" I burst out, pointing at the two of them. Oli flips me off, but Holden winks at me.

"Funnily enough, there are still some brand-new sex toys in the cupboard, and we know the count had good taste because they're all from Aunt Merideth's collection," Holden continues, ignoring my outburst. "We need to ditch anything that's not wrapped, and Harlow asked us to remove all the linens and clothes. We managed to empty the panic room completely, which reminds me, we need to get a new mattress for that gorgeous bed down there."

"How did you get it out?" Thomas asks. "I thought it was a spiral staircase leading down to the panic room. Harlow said the bed was big enough to sleep four or five adults. There's no way a mattress that big would go up a spiral staircase."

Finally recovered from his embarrassment, Oli jumps in. "It came apart in individual sections, which made it easy for the two of us to carry it up and put it in the elevator. When we got down to the public floor, we just hauled it over the balcony and dropped it into the dumpster. I took a photo of it on my phone before we pulled it apart. I'm going to call around and find someone to make us a new one."

"Oh, Declan, how do you think Princess will cope if we get another cat?" Holden asks our big brother, and his eyebrows jump in surprise.

"Why do we need another cat?" He sounds a little disgruntled, like his Princess isn't good enough.

"Well, we seem to have a bit of a mouse problem. I just thought if we got another cat, it might help fix that."

Declan grumbles, "Princess is a good mouser, but I guess we could get another cat. All of her kittens are already promised to families, so we would have to buy one."

"I know she is, but she's an inside-only cat, and I think we're going to need one who likes to go outside as well. In fact, we may need two. It's a lot of acreage, and the zoo is going to have feed that will attract rodents as well." Holden's trying to use his gentle voice, but there's a little undercurrent of laughter like he's trying to hide his opinion that our brother is being a little dramatic.

"What if we go to a rescue shelter and get one or two from there? We could use it as an opportunity to give adult cats a new home. You know they're a lot less likely to get adopted than the kittens are."

"Oh yeah, Harlow will love that idea," I chime in, feeling relaxed and happy while surrounded by my brothers. The only thing that could make this better would be Jax and Harlow being here, with the latter tucked in next to me.

"Alright, shall I leave that with you then, big brother?" Holden looks at Declan, who nods, taking out his phone to make a note. "Great, so Oli and I still have the costume wardrobe, the linens, the mattress, the cage bed, and the sex pit to deal with."

"Cage bed? Sex pit?" I sit up straighter now. "Did you happen to take any photos? I would love to see what you mean."

Oli grins and pulls out his phone. "Yeah, I did. I knew you guys might want to have a look."

"How about you drop them onto my laptop?" Declan suggests, opening it up. Of course Dec would bring his laptop to a drinking session with his brothers. "Then we can all get a look at the room without having to gather around your phone."

The two of them busy themselves with doing that when Tom's phone rings.

"Is it Harlow?" Holden asks, looking hopeful, but Tom shakes his head. "Nah, it's just Jake. Let me take this. Don't start the show without me." He points at the laptop.

My eyes follow him as he wanders away, curious to hear what his spy friend is calling for, but my mind skips back a beat.

"Hey, speaking of cats... What's happening

with the big cats? Who's looking after them while Harlow is on her cruise?" I ask Declan as a photo of Nyx pops up on his screen while we wait for Oli to send him the photos.

"Doug and Clem have got it all under control. Both of them came to the gala, but we had a driver take them home at the end of the night. Security made sure that they had one guard assigned to the cage the whole night to ensure no one was on the premises just in case." Declan types a few commands on his keyboard before Oli's photos air drop in.

"That's good, one less thing for Harlow to worry about when she's away. Hopefully, she will actually relax and enjoy herself." Holden brushes his hair back as the photos pop up on the laptop screen.

"Hurry up, Thomas," I call out, not taking my eyes away from the screen, my imagination already running wild at the thought of what Harlow and I can get up to in that room. I shift in my seat, trying to give my rapidly hardening dick some room. When I look up, Oli is smirking at me since the little shit obviously knows what I'm thinking. I flip him off and look for Tom, wondering what the hell is taking him so long.

Thomas

"Hey, Jake, what's up?" I say into the phone, moving away from my brothers. As I wait for him to reply, I start pacing up and down the length of the bar.

"Thomas, I've got some information on that name you gave me, and you are *not* going to believe what I was able to dig up. Peitre Baciu is none other than Count Bucătaru's nephew."

I stop my pacing at this revelation. "I thought he had no other family left except the twins," I say to my colleague, and I can practically feel him shrug through the phone.

"The Baciu family moved to the US when they were young. His father was Bucătaru's younger brother, and he and his wife and Peitre's two sisters were killed in a house fire when Peitre was eighteen. He disappeared. The fire was started under suspicious circumstances that local authorities later ruled arson. Peitre was the main suspect for a while, but when he never resurfaced, they ruled that whoever had set the fire must have taken Peitre and that he was most likely dead too."

"Well, that's shitty police work," I grunt.

He snorts. "Tell me about it. I think they just wanted to close the case and be done with it. I have a feeling they may have been pressured from higher up."

"Or Bucătaru greased some wheels. I'll ask Dad

if he knows anything about it. I'm assuming Peitre is around his and Dragos' age."

"He's actually eight years older than your dad. Eventually, there were whispers that he was alive. Rumors say that he became the go-to man for his uncle's business dealings on the East Coast. It was too hard for them to physically get a pin on the guy, and the arson case was never reopened for whatever reason. Possibly because they saw the potential openings for other charges? Who knows. He seemed to be cutting a bloody path through the local gangs and cartels to put his uncle's business on top, but then the uncle disappeared. Peitre was not as popular as he thought he was, and all of the people he was dealing with closed up business with him once he lost Bucătaru's backing.

"He then reappears years later. What he was doing in the meantime, no one can work out. Maybe he wasn't stateside, but who knows? This time, he's pledging himself to the Silent Brothers, the MC you visited on the East Coast. He was set to pledge to them, but the MC lost its old president just as he was about to, and he didn't like the direction the new one decided to take the club. Needless to say, he parted ways with them."

"So the count and his son disappear, and all of his business contacts don't trust the nephew, so that income dries up. Peitre has nothing, and I can't imagine he's particularly popular after killing his way to the top. Where did he go after the MC?"

"Well, I couldn't find any record of Peitre Baciu after that. I thought maybe he had changed his name and gotten a new identity given the lack of a paper trail. I did some digging, poked at a few old informants, and what do you think I found?"

"Just tell me, asshole. Stop fucking with me," I growl.

"Okay, don't get your boxers in a bunch. Peitre Baciu became Peter Bunch. He dabbled in some petty crimes, enough to support himself but not enough to appear on any big agencies' radars. For some unknown reason, he decided to go straight for the last three years. He was employed by Chuck Boston as one of his riders/groomers."

I feel my heart start to pound, and my free hand curls into a fist, tension immediately riding my whole body. "Fuck, that can't be a coincidence."

"No, I wouldn't think it was. I've passed the information on to the detectives that were in charge of Harlow's mom's murder case. They were looking for a female suspect, but this is at least another piece to the puzzle despite us not knowing where it fits."

"Yeah, but now we have more gaps to fill than we do pieces, and I just can't see how they all fit together." I need to get him off the phone, so I can tell the guys what he discovered. Then I need to call Dad and Chuck and tell the guys.

But when I look back at my brothers, I can see they've left the worries behind for the moment, and

I don't want to break the mood. I'll give them this afternoon, then first thing tomorrow, I'll tell them what I've learned. There's nothing that can be done about it now as far as they're concerned.

"Well, keep me up to date if you learn anything more." I say goodbye to Jake and hang up, then I pull up Dad and Chuck's numbers, conferencing them into one call so I don't have to repeat myself.

When Dad answers, he's laughing, though I have a distinct feeling that won't last long. "Hey, Tom, did you know you're calling both me and Chuck at the same time?" I can hear Chuck in the background, so I disconnect his line.

"Hey, Dad, can you put me on speaker? I need Chuck to hear this."

The laughter stops, and the phone gets the echoey quality that it has when on speaker. "Okay, you've got both of us now. Is this about seeing Veronica this morning? How did that go?" Dad loses all amusement in his tone, and I shake my head even though they can't see me.

"No, that.. Well that wasn't great, but I think we've come up with a solution. Poor Forrest should be off on his trip with his wife. I'll tell you about that later. I've just spoken to Jake, and I need to fill you in on what he told me."

"Don't leave us hanging, Tom," Chuck calls out, and I lean against the bar.

"Shit, Chuck, it's about your employee Peter." I hear a sharp inhale.

"What about him? Don't tell me he's dead, too. Weeks ago, he just up and left without a word, and I've been dealing with the horses on my own ever since."

"No, he's not dead, but we did find out that Peter isn't his real name."

It's not?" Chuck sounds bewildered, and I don't blame him.

"No, Peter's real name is Peitre Baciu," I tell them both, and there's a brief silence.

"That name is familiar. Why do I know that name?" Dad asks, thinking out loud.

"He was Count Bucătaru's nephew, though I'm not sure why they had different last names."

"Oh yes, I remember Dragos telling me about them. I always thought the different last name was strange. Apparently, Bucătaru's younger brother got a woman pregnant when they were about sixteen, and their father sent them away so as not to shame the family.Dragos didn't talk about them much. Bad blood, apparently. The younger brother resented the elder Bucătaru for not standing up to their father and supporting him."

"Wait, are you telling me he's been working for me for years? But why?" Chuck sounds confused and angry.

"Well, that's the million dollar question, isn't it? Jake's working on it, but I thought I should let you both know in case either of you can remember anything Peter might have said, Chuck, that made you suspicious, or anything Dragos might have said to you, Dad, about his family."

"There's nothing that stands out immediately," Chucks says, and Dad murmurs his agreement.

"But I'll think about it some more," he promises me, and Chuck echoes the sentiment.

"Call me if you think about anything," I tell them, and we hang up.

Shoving my phone into my pocket, I look back toward my brothers who are laughing over something. My heart aches for my family and everything we're going through at the moment. The need to fill my brothers in wars with the part of me that doesn't want to cause them any more stress today. Hopefully, they understand when I tell them tomorrow why I didn't do it today. Leaning over the bar, I grab another bottle of alcohol before heading back to join my brothers in our pity party.

Chapter Eight

Jaxon

The man on the steps is dressed in jeans and a t-shirt with sneakers on his feet. He's probably the same age as my dad, but where my dad looks good for his age, this guy looks rough. His skin has that weathered, dry look about it, and he has a dark tan that tells me he spends a lot of time outside. His hair is mostly gray, with only a few black patches in it, and he looks like he hasn't shaved for a few days. But unlike the well-kept groomed stubble my brothers and I sometimes sport, his is scraggly.

Harlow's gasp tells me that she recognizes the man who beat the crap out of me. I have a million questions I'm dying to ask, but I hold my tongue. The situation here is fragile, and I don't want to ask the wrong thing which could lead to one of us getting hurt, or worse—dead.

"Peter, what the hell? You and Luke were in on this together?" she asks, trying to control her emotions, but I can hear the tears she's holding back.

The fake smile on Peter's face disappears into a scowl. "That idiot son of mine went rogue. He killed your mother, then followed you out here. He thought he was protecting you. You were never supposed to be involved in this. If he had left your mother alone, you'd still be in Connecticut, blissfully unaware. Then the idiot started stalking you. He fucked everything up, so he had to go."

Oh wow, that was *not* what I was expecting to hear.

"Luke was your son?" She sounds blown away by this information.

"Dad..." Raquel walks over to me and places herself in my lap. Disgust rolls through me as she rubs against my body, but I play along, smiling. "You told me that I could have Jaxon! When is this going to be over so we can get on with our lives?"

A look of disgust washes over Peter's face. "You stupid bitch, get off of him. You can't have him! He's your cousin."

"What?" I can't believe what I just heard. My cousin!? I had a relationship with my cousin? Shaking my body the best I can, I try to dislodge her. "Fucking get off me. Did you know this?" I ask her, nausea curdling my stomach when I think about the things we did.

"No, of course not." She's staring at her dad with as much disgust as I am.

"Relax," Cecelia drawls as she steps forward. "You're not blood cousins. Peter is our step-dad. He came into our lives just after Raquel was born."

Oh thank fuck for that.

Peter smirks like he enjoyed inflicting that mental torture on me. "But I *am* your relative. The count was my uncle. My father was his younger brother, and I'm here to collect my dues. I lost everything when he disappeared. You owe me!" He points between me and my sister while Jacinta and I look at each other in shock. I can't believe this asshole is a blood relative. Sounds like all the men in our family were assholes. Maybe Dad was too, but he hid it better. *Holy shit, that means that Harlow's stalker was our cousin, too. Everything she's gone through is our fucking fault in one way or another.*

"What do you want?" Jacinta asks. "There's gold in the vault. Take that and let us go."

Peter scoffs, turning his attention to my sister. "I wanted my product, the guns and the drugs, but you fucked that up by getting the authorities involved. The gold is useless to me, so no, I want something way more important than that."

He breaks off as the door to the top of the stairs opens again. Turning, he waits for whoever is about to join us. "Ah, here comes the rest of the family reunion. This is going to be so much fun." He sounds slightly unhinged, and I know I shouldn't look away from him, but my attention can't help but be drawn to the slow tap of new footsteps on the stairs. They've certainly got a flair for the dramatic. When they get to the bottom, they hover in the shadows for a moment, then I hear Harlow gasp again.

"Mom?" She sounds confused, and there are tears streaming down her face. I guess Harlow somehow still loved her even though the woman was a bitch. But when the woman steps out of the shadows, the tears slow. "Wait, you're not my mom."

"Of course I'm not that junkie whore. Peter's idiot son killed her, and you identified her body. I thought you were supposed to be smart, Harlow. Maybe your mom's drug use while pregnant with you did actually do some damage." The woman's voice is harsh, and she sneers at Harlow.

"What the fuck is going on? Can one of you please explain who you are and what the fuck you want?" My sister sounds terrified and exasperated, but the four people not tied to a chair just look smug.

"I guess we could start at the beginning. I mean, we have nothing but time, don't we? No one is expecting you back for a couple more days, and we'll be long gone by then," the woman says.

Cecelia groans. "Fine, but I'm sitting down if I

have to listen to it all again." She plonks herself down on one of the bottom steps and examines her fingernails in boredom.

"Just to clarify, Jaxon and I definitely are not blood related?" Raquel asks the woman, and she scrunches her face up.

"No, who told you that shit? I wouldn't have asked you to seduce him if you were. I might not have a lot of morals, but I draw the line at incest."

Raquel points to Peter. "He did."

The woman rolls her eyes. "Jesus, Peter. For a fifty-seven year-old man, you're a fucking idiot."

"It's fun fucking with them. You should have seen Jaxon's face."

"Well, I want what you promised me. You said I could have Jaxon," Raquel simpers before she plants herself back on my lap. I hide the revulsion I feel since the woman is closely watching me.

"You can have him long enough to create an heir. Once you're carrying the heir to the Bucătaru fortune, we won't need him anymore."

"No! I want to keep him." Raquel's voice takes on a stubborn tone. I can't see her face, but I'm assuming she's pouting. The woman waves her off.

"We can discuss it later, but for now I want to tell my niece here a story." My head swings to look at Harlow, and her mouth has dropped open in shock.

"You're my aunt! Why did my mom never say anything about you?"

Harlow's aunt rolls her eyes. "Diane never forgave me for chasing off Brad. How was I to know he was a billionaire? I just thought he was some beach bum college grad who had no prospects." She sighs, a faraway look in her eyes like she's lost in memories.

"Where shall I start? I guess I could go back a little further to really set the story since you're such a *captive* audience. Diane and I grew up in Hartford, in that very trailer she used to live in. Our mom was a waitress, and our dad had died when Diane was small. Mom worked hard to feed and clothe us, but by the time I was ten, I was often left alone to look after Diane even though I was only three years older than her. As I got older, I swore I wouldn't live like my mom did, struggling day to day, sometimes bringing a man home so that she could pay the rent and keep food on the table for us. Eventually, she decided that earning money on her back was easier than waitressing. Thankfully, she didn't bring her customers home most of the time."

Raquel, on my lap, pulls out her phone and starts playing a game. She's obviously heard all this before. I desperately want to shove her off, but I don't want to draw any extra attention to us while this woman is telling her story.

Peter's phone rings, and he brushes past Cecelia and goes upstairs to talk uninterrupted.

"Anyway, I decided I wanted to be an actress and left home as soon as I turned eighteen. I'd been working a job for a couple of years and saved as many tips as I could, so as soon as I had enough for a plane ticket, I was gone. My mother disowned me and told me never to return. She might not have been the best mother, but I guess she cared in some way. She said some things that I brushed off then, but I admit now that I was naive and deluded. I had no special skills, and although I was pretty, I had no talent. Eventually, I had to make a decision. Come home and grovel to my mother or earn some money on my back. I refused to grovel to that woman, so I got a job with an escort agency. That's when I came across Count Bucătaru for the first time. I was hired to work at one of his parties. He liked the look of me, and I became one of his 'girls.'"

She's been walking back and forth across the room, occasionally looking us over, but it's almost like she's telling the story to herself. Both Harlow and Jacinta are riveted, but even though I'm listening, my eyes gaze around the room, looking for a way out. But then she stops, and a strange look comes upon her face. It's almost like fear, but it's quickly replaced by anger as her fists clench.

"Being one of his girls wasn't all it was cracked up to be. See, by then, Bucătaru had quite depraved tastes, and we were his favorite outlet." She pauses and shudders before shaking herself.

"So, when I found a chance to escape, I did. I raided his stash of drugs, took a chunk of cash from the safe in the sex room, and came back to Hartford. By then, Diane had graduated highschool, and she was excited to see her big sister regardless. I never told her the truth, you see. I just told her that I lived in a lavish mansion with a rich man and everything was awesome. She had no clue that I needed drugs to get through most days. Turns out my mother and I weren't that different, and when she discovered I could provide her with recreational drugs, she welcomed me home with wide arms." The woman grimaces. "Diane was such a fucking goodie two shoes. She had a job working as a PA for that bitch Melinda and was good friends with her and her husband. And she was dating Brad, who she'd met through Chuck. Her life was good, and she had somehow done well for herself despite being left behind with our mother. I *hated* seeing that. How dare she! But because I was her big sister, who she worshiped, it didn't take much to convince her to party with us. She was always desperate for me to approve of her."

Raquel wiggles impatiently on my lap, and I grunt at the pain in my knees. They hadn't been spared when I had been beaten earlier. "Oh, for fuck's sake, Raquel. Get off of him and go sit with your sister," her mother growls, yanking her off of me and pushing her toward the steps.

"Ouch, do you have to be such a bitch?" Raquel sulks as she makes herself comfortable next to Cecelia. Harlow's aunt rolls her eyes and turns her back to her daughters, facing us again, before continuing her story.

"Diane and I looked very much alike, and one day after she had passed out on the couch, she got a message from Brad, telling her he wanted to see her. I messaged back, pretending to be her, saying that I was drunk and he should come get me. She'd never brought him around to our place for a reason."

"When he got there, it was dark. Our porch light was broken, so when I went out to greet him, he thought I was Diane. She hadn't told him that she had a sister, of course. As much as my little sister loved me, there was a certain sense of... self-preservation at play. She wouldn't have wanted to scare him away by letting him see our home or knowing the truth about our mother or her wayward sister. I tried to seduce him, but he kept pushing me off, saying he wouldn't take advantage of her when she was drunk. Little did he know that she was high the last few times they'd been together. I got angry and told him I never wanted to see him again, screaming at him to get out of my life. He left, telling me he would return the next day when I was sober."

Peter comes back downstairs, and she pauses. "Julia, I need to go out. I'll be back in a little while. Don't start anything without me."

She waves a hand at him. "Don't worry, I've still got a bit of story to tell." He pulls her to him and kisses her passionately. Raquel gags, and Jacinta,

Harlow, and Cecelia all look as grossed out as I feel when he starts feeling her up in front of us all.

"Fuck, I can't wait to get access to my uncle's sex room. The things I'm going to do to you," Peter growls at Julia, who turns away from him, hiding the terror that has risen in her eyes at his words. He leaves, oblivious to her feelings.

"I need a drink before we continue this. Cecelia, get us a drink and some party favors. I think everyone will be a little more relaxed if we indulge."

Cecelia huffs. "Fine, Mom, but can you hurry it up? This trip down memory lane is nauseating." She follows her stepfather back upstairs while Julia looks around the room.

"I thought there were more chairs down here," she says to Raquel.

"There are a couple of plastic ones in the bathroom," she replies, not looking up from her phone.

"Well, don't just sit there being useless. Get me one. And grab one for your sister, too." Raquel gets off the step and flounces toward the bathroom, grumbling as she goes.

Harlow gasps again. "If you're my aunt and they're your daughters, that means Cecelia and Raquel are actually my cousins."

Raquel appears, carrying a stack of plastic chairs, and sneers at her. "Wow, you can put two and two together."

She puts the chairs down and separates the

three of them before slouching down in one. I breathe a sigh of relief that she doesn't resituate herself on my lap.

Julia takes a seat and smiles at us, the crazy in her eyes plain to see. "Now, where was I?"

"You told Brad to go away," Jacinta points out helpfully. I smother a snort of laughter. Despite our terrible situation, my sister cannot resist a juicy story, and this is certainly one of those.

"Oh yes, so after he left, I made myself look ravished, ripped my shirt, messed up my hair, and smeared my lipstick. Then I stumbled back inside loudly enough to wake my useless sister. I told her that Brad had seduced me, and she was still fucked up enough to believe it." Her smile is filled with a sick pleasure, but then it drops, and I see that glimpse of fear in her eyes again.

"But that night, the count's men found me and dragged me back to L.A. where he punished me for my disobedience."

"But what has that got to do with me or Jaxon or Harlow? Why start this vendetta or whatever this is? Why did you try to kill her?" Jacinta just doesn't know when to keep her mouth shut, and I don't miss the glare Julia shoots her way, clearly not appreciating the interruption.

"I was friends with your mom for a little while. Did you know that?" She ignores Jacinta's outburst and turns to me. I mean, I can kind of believe it. She seems like a bit of a terrible person, and with the way she keeps bouncing around, she comes off as slightly unhinged.

"She was one of his girls too, but when he saw that his son had taken an interest in her, he made her focus on him. He thought he could control Dragos through her. Carmen was beautiful and popular, and Dragos never knew she was a whore." She thinks about it and shrugs. "Or maybe he did and just didn't care. Anyway, she told me that she and Dragos were going to run away together. They had a plan. He was going to steal some gold from the vault, and they were going to use the tunnels to get away."

"So what, you betrayed your friend to get back in the count's good books?" Harlow blurts out, and Julia looks at her niece, a smug smile on her face.

"Hey, in this world, it's every woman for themselves. I told the count, and he and I were there to intercept them. He sent Carmen back upstairs, telling her he would deal with her later. The vault was already open, and I couldn't believe what I saw in there. All the drugs and guns and pretty, pretty expensive things… not to mention the stack of gold. While they were busy arguing, I picked up one of the guns and shot them both. Then I shoved as much as I could in a bag, closed the vault behind me, and made my way out, following one of the tunnels."

"So you killed my dad and grandfather?" I say to her.

She grins. "You bet your ass I did."

That's interesting. She obviously doesn't know we only found one body. We didn't make that public.

"And I guess you thought you could come back whenever... until you realized you needed the combination and some blood." I smirk at her, and she jumps to her feet and starts pacing.

"Yes, the stuff I stole lasted for quite a few years, but then it ran out. I still knew how to get in through the tunnels, so I decided to come back and help myself to more. It was easy enough to come at night when Vincent was occupied. That's when I realized how badly I had fucked up."

Just then, Cecelia comes back downstairs, carrying a tray. She has three bottles of beer on it and a bowl of potato chips.

"Oh good, I'm starving." Julia grabs a bottle off the tray, and the three of them set about having a picnic.

"Seriously?" my sister exclaims, but Harlow isn't paying attention. She's lost in thought, and I would love to know what is going through her mind. God knows I've got a lot going through mine right now.

Chapter Nine

Declan

"Fucking hell, I'm too old for this shit," I mumble as I roll over in bed, trying to block out the morning light blazing through the open windows.

My mouth feels like I ate sawdust, my head throbs, and my eyes are sensitive to the light. I freeze when I feel a body next to mine, and my heart starts to beat violently with the question of who's in bed next to me. Surely I didn't cheat on Harlow. I hadn't been interested in any women for a long time before she came into my life. I certainly wouldn't have fucked up the best thing to happen to me just because I drank a little too much.

I slowly move my body away from whoever it is, but I don't get far before a hairy arm and leg are thrown over my body, and I'm spooned from behind. Kai's mumbling in his sleep, easing my heart, stopping it from jumping out of my chest. I relax for a moment before I throw his heavy limbs off me.

"Get off me, you idiot. I'm not your girl-friend." I swing my legs off the hotel bed and stagger to the bathroom. I take a piss, and when I've washed my hands, I cup them, filling them with water to throw over my face. The cold splash helps a little, but I know that the next thing I'm doing is placing an order with room service. I look at myself in the mirror over the sink and grimace. I'm wearing only my boxers, and my eyes are bloodshot red, but it's the bandage across the top of my chest that really makes me take notice. Fucking hell, did I hurt myself? I'm wracking my brain, but then a foggy memory comes to life. My eyes widen as I rip the bandage off.

"Oh fucking hell, I'm never drinking again," I mutter as I take in the new tattoo sitting above my Princess tattoo.

"You know, even as drunk as he was last night, he did a really good job of that," Kai says, pushing past me to take a piss.

I run my finger over the stylized words. Kai's right; Harlow's name is perfect and now perma-nently etched above my heart.

"She's never going to let me live this down," I moan as I go back into the bedroom, pulling on a pair of sweats and padding into the living area of our suite.

Picking up the phone, I place an order with room service. I'm just putting the phone back in its cradle when the door to the suite opens. Thomas steps in, red and sweaty, so I can tell he's already been making use of the gym. I grunt a hello and throw myself down on the couch.

"How can you be exercising so early after drinking so much last night?" I mumble, throwing my head back, closing my eyes, and putting an arm over them to block out the rest of the painful light.

"I drank plenty of water, and the run helped me sweat out the remains, even if it was painful," he snaps, obviously not doing as well as I had thought. Glad I'm not suffering alone.

"I ordered coffee and breakfast. By the time you shower, it should be here," I tell him, and he nods, leaving me to do as I bid.

Kai stumbles out of the room we shared and starts to sit down, but I hold up a hand. "Can you grab my phone for me? I think it's on the dining table." He marches over to the table and picks up two cells before he finds the right one. He brings it back to me and collapses onto the couch, assuming the same position I did.

"I'm never drinking again," he groans as I power up my phone. I had turned it off last night, not wanting anyone to interrupt our pity party for Kai and Thomas, but now I need to get back to real life. A few messages make themselves known, and there's a missed call from Dad, but nothing from Harlow or either of the twins.

Frowning, I'm about to return Dad's phone call when Oliver comes bounding out followed by Holden. While the latter is a little slower, neither of them look hungover at all.

Kai sits up a little and waves a finger between the two of them "What kind of magical fuckery is this? Why are the two of you not hungover?"

Oliver throws himself onto the couch next to Kai and plants a kiss on his cheek. "Because, brother of mine, Holden and I have more shit to do today if we want things ready before Harlow gets back from her cruise."

Holden takes a seat on one of the other sofas. "Yeah, so, Oli and I were smart enough to stop drinking early, and we switched to water. It's why your tattoo looks like it does and not a shit storm. I wouldn't have let him tattoo you if he was as drunk as you all were." I go to ask something, but he holds his hand up. "And before you ask, I did tell you not to do it. You insisted. I figure Oli can do a quick cover-up if you don't want it."

When he mentions covering it up, my heart skips a beat. I quickly shake my head, and an amused grin crosses his face.

"Yeah, that's what I thought."

Just then, someone knocks on the door, and

Thomas returns freshly dressed in jeans and t-shirt, rubbing a towel over his wet hair.

"That was quick," I comment as he saves me from getting up to open the door. Instead of the room service I'd expected, our dad is standing on the other side, looking extremely agitated. What in the world has happened to make him tug at his hair like he's going to make himself bald.

"Why haven't any of you got your damn phones on?" he snaps, which is unusual for him.

"Hey, I thought you and Chuck were going off on a road trip yesterday?" I ask.

"No, we had to delay it. We were going today, but I just got a phone call from a very agitated cruise captain, blasting me for how unprofessional it was to not bother showing up."

Dad's announcement wakes me up more than any cup of coffee could have, and I can see it has the same effect on my brothers. My heart races in fear and my stomach rolls, all the alcohol I drank last night threatening to make a reappearance.

"What do you mean not bothering to show up?" Thomas asks, throwing the towel to the side, his red hair sticking up in all angles.

"Harlow and the twins never boarded the cruise after the gala. Something has happened. Mom and Dad are calling around to hospitals, checking their newly admitted patients, but I don't think they're going to have any luck."

I see Oliver reach for Holden's hand out of the corner of my eye.

"They've been taken, haven't they?" Kai's voice is flat as he says the one thing none of us wanted to hear.

"I think they may have been, yes," Dad confirms, and the room bursts into sound, my already pounding head spiking in pain at the noise. Thomas hurries over to the dining table and grabs his phone, calling someone and shouting instructions. Kai, Oli, and Holden are peppering Dad with questions, but I can tell he has no answers. All I can do is sit here in shock, my complete helplessness pinning me to the spot.

No, this can't be happening to me. I can't be losing people I love *again*. I struggled to recover after I lost my parents, and Dad, Nana, and Poppy helped me through that, but if we lose Harlow and the twins, who's going to help all of us this time?

The next hour passes in a whirlwind of conversation, with Dad and Tom telling us about their conversation the previous evening. By the time we've all cooled down enough not to hit our brother for delaying sharing the news of Peter's identity, I'm at a complete loss. The action fades away around me as I retreat into myself, something I haven't done since I was a child. Not since the twins arrived on our doorstep and I became a big brother, charged with looking after them and protecting them. Dad knew it was just what I needed to come out of my self-imposed shell. But now I can see that his trust was misplaced. I failed to protect them. I failed to protect the one person I love more than my family.

I am not worthy of any of them.

Chapter Ten

Harlow

While the three women take a break, drinking their beer and munching on their chips, my mind races with everything I know so far. I have an aunt and cousins, the twins have an uncle, and all of them are cunts. I check on my boyfriend and his sister, and both of them are staring daggers at our kidnappers. I don't blame them. I'm just glad those daggers aren't aimed at me… yet. My aunt killed Jaxon and Jacinta's dad and grandfather. How can they look at me the same way now that they know that? The moments as I wait to see what I'll find in their eyes drag on.

Jaxon must be able to feel my eyes on him because he turns, slowly so as not to draw anyone's attention. I brace myself, but when his eyes meet mine, there's no resentment, just worry and love. I let out a small sigh of relief. Now that I'm reassured about us, I can concentrate on what she just disclosed.

"So then what happened?" Jacinta frowns at me as if she can will me to shut up, but I need to know the rest of the story.

"I left LA and laid low for a while. Eventually, I met the girls' dad, and we had them. Brad returned home the minute Dragos and his father were reported as missing. He and Diane never spoke again after the night I interfered. I learned that from my mom, who was happy to report things to me when I sent her money. But then Diane found out she was pregnant. She tried to stay sober, but she was too weak. Eventually, that fucking bitch fired her and reported her to child services. Diane lost custody of you. I think she was relieved, to be honest, since Mom said she didn't seem to care. It was about four years later that I saw Brad being interviewed on TV, and I discovered how badly I'd fucked up with him. The girls' dad had died by then, and I was struggling, so I gave them to his mother to raise while I tried to sort my life out."

Jacinta snorts with amusement. "What are we up to now? That's your second major fuck-up. Or technically, I guess it was your first."

Julia screams and lunges for Jacinta, backhanding her across the face. Her lip, which had stopped bleeding, drips blood again. I shout, help-lessly watching as my aunt hits her again.

"Keep your fucking hands off my sister, you crazy bitch," Jaxon shouts as well, but she's willfully deaf to our demands.

"Aunt Julia," I call firmly, drawing her attention away from my sister who has tears streaming down her face. "So they're younger than I am?" I ask about her daughters, trying to distract her from Jacinta. I'm surprised to hear that, especially about Cecelia.

"Yes, Cecelia is only about a year younger and Raquel two."

Which would put them at twenty-five and twenty-three respectively, considering my twenty-sixth birthday is only a few weeks away. With every-thing that's happened, I had forgotten.

"Did you tell my mom about Brad?" is the next thing I ask, hoping to keep her attention on me.

Julia is breathing heavily, but it starts to slow down. "You were such a pretty, happy baby. You were about three when I returned. You just happened to be with Diane for her weekend when I came to see her. But your mom was so addicted to everything by then, and I couldn't get her to focus on what I was saying. She had convinced herself what I'd said was the truth and didn't care. She wanted nothing to do with him and wasn't going to tell him about his daughter. I left then and never returned after that. I had planned to tell Brad about his daughter, but when I returned to LA, I accidentally ran into Carmen and discovered the twins." She looks between Jaxon and Jacinta, smirking with unrestrained glee.

"Your mother was as much of a whore as Diane by then, but she wasn't as much of an addict. When Dragos and Count Bucătaru disappeared, she was considered a suspect for a brief moment, but they let her go since she had nothing and nowhere to go. She had a few bits of jewelry and a car that Dragos had given her, but she had to sell them so she could put a roof over her head. The count's girls all had to return to working for the escort agency they had originally come from. When Carmen was working, one of the other whores watched her children for her. I ran into her when I went to visit another friend that worked for the agency. I knew immediately that the twins were Dragos and thought my luck had finally changed."

"You saw the kids as your ticket to getting back into the vault," I say flatly.

"You bet your ass I did, and it didn't take much to convince Carmen. She was weak like your mom, Harlow. So every week, I would take blood from the twins, then I would spend hours in that vault trying different combinations. But then that bitch got cold feet. I was taking more and more blood each week, and I think she was worried that I was going to kill them, which would have been stupid because I needed them... or at least one of them. Blood replenishes itself fast enough that there was really no cause for worry. Anyway…" She waves a hand in the air like she's brushing off Carmen's stupidity. "The next time I went to draw blood, they weren't there. She had given them to Brad, then done a runner. Gone." She starts to pace agitatedly again.

"Here, Mom, you're starting to get stressed out. Come take a hit of this." Raquel waves a straw at her. While we had been engrossed in the story, Cecelia and Raquel had been snorting coke. Great… not only are they crazy, they're junkies.

"I can't believe you were Dad's PA," Jacinta spits at my cousin who stands up.

"God, I'm sick of looking at their faces. Can we take a break? I want to enjoy my high, not listen to them. I can't stand the sight of the spoiled bitches," Cecelia whines, and Raquel throws her head back, dragging the back of her hand across her nose.

Julia's eyes light up at the idea. "You go. Your dad will be back soon, and he was bringing some of the boys to party. Need to keep our future clients happy. Why don't the two of you put on something pretty for them to look at?" Julia turns her back to them, missing the grimace they exchange. A tiny prick of sympathy hits me before I remember they're responsible for me being tied to a chair. Fuck them, I hope someone fucks them with a cactus.

The two of them disappear upstairs, and Julia turns her attention back to us.

"I was livid when I found out that Carmen had given the twins to Brad. I was fucked. No blood, and no money left. No point in telling Brad about his real child now that he had adopted all the others. Why the fuck would he care about having one more mouth to feed and nose to wipe? So I was left with no choice but to do what I do best."

I can see that Jacinta is dying to make some kind of snarky comment, but she keeps her mouth closed. I guess she did learn.

"I drifted around, not staying anywhere for long, and it wasn't until about ten years later that I remembered Count Bucătaru had a brother on the East Coast, and he had a son. The son, being the count's nephew, might have been enough of a blood match. If he happened to know the combination—I don't know, maybe that shit was passed down through the generations— that could be my ticket. So I headed back to the East Coast, and can you imagine my surprise when I found him trying to patch in with the Silent Brothers MC? He was even fucking around with your whore of a mother. Diane always had all the luck even though she was too fucking stupid to know how to use it."

This story is so fucking complicated, and I don't see what I have to do with any of this. But I stay quiet and let Julia continue to tell her story.

"I avoided my sister and Harlow that time and cornered Peitre one day when he wasn't with Diane. Unfortunately, he had no clue about the vault under the house, but he was ready to jump at the chance of breaking into it. We returned to LA and broke into the vault. We had planned to approach the trust and claim the inheritance, but when we tried his blood, it didn't work. Turns out his mother was a lying whore, and he wasn't a *real* member of the family line. So not only could we not claim the inheritance, we couldn't get into the vault."

"Wow, how many fuck-ups are we up to now? It's like a long life of clusterfucks, isn't it, Jaxon?"

Oh my god. Jaxon and I look at Jacinta in disbelief. It's like she's deliberately trying to draw my aunt's fury. What is she doing? Some sort of self-sacrificing shit?

But this time my aunt just ignores her. "We had no other choice but to try and make it on our own. Peitre and I came back to the East Coast, I took my children back from their grandma, and he got custody of his son from his ex. For a while, we were semi-legit. Well, as legit as we could be. Peitre still had a few contacts from when he'd worked for his uncle, but they were the small fish. We managed to get by."

"Did you two have anything to do with my mom trying to reconnect with Jacinta when we were about sixteen?" Jaxon asks my aunt, and a growl escapes her lips.

"No, that bitch had hooked up with another gang, and they just wanted access to the mansion. They wanted to steal a whole heap of shit. Like my sister, your mother was full of small, useless dreams." She looks down at her fingernails before looking up at Jaxon. "Do you know how I know that?"

There's an almost gleeful smile on her face when he shakes his head. "I tortured it out of her before I put a bullet in her brain. Stupid bitch had made access to the two of you that much harder, and she deserved to be punished for making my life more difficult." Jacinta gasps, and I see Jaxon's hands tighten on his chair handles. Julia starts to chuckle, which devolves into maniacal laughter. Jacinta has tears streaming down her face, while her brother's jaw is tense with emotion. He keeps his face blank, not wanting to give her more ammunition.

The door at the top of the stairs bangs once more, and the sound of heels on the stairs echoes through the basement. When Cecelia gets to the bottom, gone are the casual jeans and t-shirt she had been rocking, and in their place is a slinky black cocktail dress and four-inch heels. Her long chestnut hair has been tied up in a sleek updo, and her face is made up with smoky eyes and blood red lips.

"Mom, Peter's home, and he's brought his friends." She doesn't sound too thrilled about that, and her body is tight with tension. Julia breaks off her crazy laughing and stands up.

"Excellent, it's all coming to a head now. It

won't be long." She rubs her hands together in a parody of every damn Disney villain out there.

She goes to leave, but I can't let her go. I need her to finish this. "But I still don't get any of this! I don't understand what any of this has to do with me. Why did Luke kill my mother? Why did he stalk me? Please, I need to know."

"You tell her. I have to get changed too." My aunt waves at my cousin, who loudly sighs before taking a seat on one of the plastic chairs and elegantly crossing her legs. Julia disappears upstairs, singing quietly to herself.

"We lived with my dad's mother until I was about thirteen. We were happy, and we had good childhoods. My dad's family was fairly well off, but it didn't matter to my mother that she was taking us away from a life that would've been better than what she and Peter could provide. Anyway, it broke something in Raquel, being torn from the life we had known and thrust into the uncertainty of our mom and *step-dad's* schemes. We went from steady, normal lives to moving from town to town, going wherever Mom or Peter could run a scam. Luke lived with us too, but there was always something off about him. I'm pretty sure he would steal our underwear, and he was always trying to catch us naked in our bedrooms or our bathroom. We ended up asking for locks on the door. For as many flaws as my mom has, she did that for us, at least."

Cecelia reaches into the top of the dress, pulls a

joint and a lighter from her cleavage, and lights it up, drawing deeply before slowly exhaling.

"The three of us spent the next five or six years listening to them rant whenever they had too much to drink or were high, scheming about how they were going to get access to you two." She waves her joint between the twins. "That's how I ended up working for your dad and Raquel for you, Jaxon. The documents and resumes and references were all high-end forgeries. Raquel was easily hired by HR, but I had to be interviewed by your dad, and I just knew he wasn't going to hire me, so that's when I blackmailed him. If I had returned home without a job, Peter would have killed me— just like he did with Luke. I'd seen Peter *discipline* his son often enough whenever he disappointed him. It was only a matter of time before things with them went too far, and Peter cared about us even less, if that was possible, considering we weren't his children."

"Okay, that explains you and Raquel, but how did Peter and Luke come to be working for Chuck?" Not sure why, but Jacinta's doing a better job keeping her tone in check with Cecelia. For all the shit that woman has wrought within our family, you'd think she'd be spitting venom at her too. But no, she's managed to pull herself together so that we can continue to get every bit of information we can.

Cecelia sighs. "Like I said, Luke was weird, and

my mom's little obsession with Harlow didn't go unnoticed."

"Obsession?"

"If the twins didn't work out, she was going to kidnap you and ransom you to Brad. You were this back-up plan that she couldn't get out of her head even though she had her doubts about it."

I can't stop the shudder that rolls over me at Cecelia's matter-of-fact statement. She's so blasé talking about kidnapping and ransom.

"Anyway, Mom decided you needed to be watched, so she sent Luke and Peter to find a foothold in the Bostons' household. You were in your third year at college, and she was worried you'd burn out or meet someone and disappear before you could be of use."

Even though I'm getting my question answered, I don't feel any better. It's honestly making me feel even more frustrated. I had always sensed something was wrong with them, but I'd never spoken up like I should have, and… I don't know… Maybe it would've made a difference.

"When Jaxon broke up with Raquel, our mom flipped. She was worried that we were never going to access the house, so she ordered them to kidnap you. Well, little did we know, Luke had become obsessed. He killed your mom, knowing that somewhere in the heap of a trailer was your birth certificate. The pain in the ass figured that you'd be safe if you found your dad yourself, so then Mom couldn't use you against him. And it worked like a charm. Before anything could be put into place to take you, you were on your way to LA."

"Holy fuck." Jacinta's exclamation sums the situation up perfectly.

Just as I'm about to ask another question, Julia shouts down the stairs, "Cecelia, get your ass up here."

Cecelia doesn't say another thing, just stands up, puts out the joint, and walks away without a backward glance.

Chapter Eleven

Harlow

I wait a few moments to make sure none of them are returning. When no one does, I start to wriggle my body.

"Holy fuck!" Jacinta exclaims, starting to do the same thing. "Your family is off-the-rails crazy." I stop and stare at her.

"Are you freaking kidding me? Your uncle killed your cousin!" I point out, and I watch as she stops struggling and thinks about it.

"Apparently, he isn't our real uncle, so you still lose," she shoots back, and I stick my tongue out at her. She giggles a little hysterically while I go back to what I was trying to do.

"What are you doing, Harlow?" Jaxon asks, and I swing my head to look at him. It was so hard to watch Raquel drape herself all over him.

"Shut up, you asshole. You don't get to speak to her," Jacinta whisper-yells, furious with her brother. She must not have heard Jaxon apologize to me earlier.

"It's okay, Jacinta. He was just pretending." She blinks and shakes her head.

"Of course he was. Sorry, my head hurts from being hit twice."

Shit, I hope she hasn't got a concussion. "Have you got any blurry vision or dizziness?" I ask her, and she slowly shakes her head, though the wince accompanying the movement isn't very convincing.

"No, it's just pounding." I breathe a small sigh of relief. At least that's one less thing to worry about. I turn back to Jaxon, hating how he looks to be in pain.

"I don't want you pretending. I don't want her all over you. I don't think it's going to help us anyway. If he's willing to kill off his own son, then nothing Raquel wants is going to keep him from doing what he wants. It sounds like they are going to get what they want from you and be done with all of us," I quietly tell him. His eyes cloud with something—Sadness? Fear? I'm not sure what it is, but I know it's not optimism.

"I think you're right, though I'm not sure how they think they can get an heir from me without my cooperation," he mumbles, sounding disgusted, and Jacinta snorts.

"Please, brother, all they have to do is drug you

and hold Harlow or me at gunpoint. After that, you would do anything for them," Jacinta says matter of factly, and I start to struggle again. I can't let that happen because she's right.

"When Cecelia hit me and the chair fell, something broke," I say, making a point to speak as quietly as possible.

"In your arm?" Jaxon asks, trying to see what I'm doing.

"No, in the chair," I reply, and sure enough, I've wiggled enough that I can detach the back of the chair from the seat. Now that I'm no longer attached, I try to stand up, and when I do, the back piece falls out. I can pull my arms out of the ropes and unwind them from my body.

"Yes!" Jacinta cheers in a whisper. "God, I could just kiss you."

I scrunch up my nose. "No thanks, I'm happy kissing your brother."

"Good call," the siblings say in unison.

"Hurry, untie Jazzy," Jaxon urges as I bend down and pull the tape off my legs.

Scrambling out of the bindings, I move over to Jacinta and untie her. "Check if there's any way we can open the window," I tell her as I go to Jaxon. Unlike us, he's shackled with metal cuffs, which won't make this easy. I pull at them, trying to loosen them, but there's no fucking way I'm getting them open.

"God, why did they tie you up like this?" I ask him, frustrated with not having any success.

"I woke up before both of you and put up a fight. That's when Peter did this to me." He points a finger at his face. "I think I may have a cracked rib or two as well." He grimaces as he shifts like he's trying to lessen the pain. I pause for a moment and lean in, placing a kiss on his lips.

"I love you. I'm so sorry about all of this."

"It's as much my fault as it is yours," he argues as I keep trying to pull his shackles. When that doesn't work, I study his chair, looking to see if I can break it in any way, like what happened to mine.

"It's neither of your fault. That woman is bat-shit crazy," Jacinta whispers. There's another minute or two of silence, the two of us struggling with our respective missions, but then Jacinta shouts, the sound all too loud and full of joy. I cringe and look at the steps, my heart racing with panic, but no one comes to investigate.

Turning back to Jacinta, she's standing in front of an open window that's big enough for us to climb out of.

"Go, get out while you both can," Jaxon tells us. "I'll be alright on my own."

I shake my head. "No way am I leaving here to deal with all of that on your own. We'll work something out. Jazzy, you go. Get help and bring them back." She shakes her head, looking like she's about to refuse.

"Go, Jazzy," Jaxon hisses. "You might be our only hope. They only need one person with Bucătaru blood, so it's riskiest for both of us to stay here. It's almost guaranteed they'll get rid of the *spare*. Look, get to the others, but be prepared for the fact that they'll likely move us once they realize you're gone. If only we knew what they actually wanted, we might be able to guess at their next location."

"It's got to be something in the vault or in the house. Why else would they need us?" I point out to them.

I leave Jaxon to drag a chair over to under the window, shoving Jacinta at it. "Go." She dodges me and runs over to hug her brother before returning to me and doing the same.

"I love you both." A tear trickles down her face, but I shove her again so that she climbs up on the chair and boosts herself out of the window. It's a tight squeeze, which makes me almost a hundred percent sure Jaxon wouldn't fit out of it anyway. I give her a slap on the ass, and she continues to wriggle her body, getting further and further out the window. Thankfully, the opening must be on the side of a house that no one is paying attention to. I mean, why would they? They think we're still neatly tied up in our chairs.

Her feet disappear, and I step up and peer out. It's dark outside, so I have no idea what time it is. I

can't see any houses next door, but there's the occa-
sional rumble of a car coming down a nearby road.
"Go get help, Jazzy. Head for the road. Maybe you
can flag someone down." With a final glance back,
she hurries away. I wait with baited breath, but no
one shouts at her to stop, and a sigh of relief bursts
out of me when it seems like she got away.

Turning back to face the room, Jaxon's
watching me with hope in his eyes. "Did she get
away?"

"Yup," I confirm before starting a search
around the room. There's not much in here, but
maybe I can find something to jimmy his shackles
or break the chair he's sitting in. When that proves
to be a dead end, I walk into the bathroom.

"What do you think they could be after?" I ask
my boyfriend.

"I have no idea. What could be of value apart
from the items in the vault?" he calls back in a loud
whisper.

"The paintings in the house are probably worth
something, but my bet is they just want to make a
grab at the contents of the vault." I dig through a
drawer located under the sink, finding a couple of
old bobby pins at the back. Picking them up, I go
back to Jaxon. "I have no idea how to do this, but it
doesn't hurt to try." I show him what I found, and
he nods even though there's clear skepticism on his
face.

Crouching down, I slide one of the pins into the

lock holding the shackle in place on his right side. I can hear my heartbeat in my ears as I try to jimmy the lock, but after a while of trying, I sit back on my heels and look up at Jaxon, feeling helpless.

"I can't get it," I admit, and although I can see disappointment in his eyes, I know he isn't angry at me.

"Come up here," he says, so I throw the pin to the side and gently sit down on his lap, wrapping my arms around his neck and leaning my forehead against his. "I love you, Harlow Summers," he whispers before placing his lips on mine. He kisses me softly before pulling away. "I want you to go out the window and get away."

I start to shake my head, but he keeps going. "Please, if you're not here, I don't have to worry about them using you to get me to do something. I don't have to worry about them hurting you. They're crazy, but they've been playing the long game, and they think the end is near. When they come down here and find Jazzy gone, they're going to freak out. I don't want you in line for that reaction. They need me. I have the code for the vault and the blood. They don't need you. Who do you think they're going to take their anger out on?"

"No way. I'm not leaving you. I'm going to see if I can creep upstairs and look for the key. Or something. They've got guests. They're busy and distracted, and I bet if we wait a little longer, their minds will be fogged with alcohol and drugs. They were already high before they left."

"Don't forget about Peter. He wasn't," Jaxon warns me, and I huff.

"Did you not notice the track lines on his arms? I know a junkie when I see one, and if he isn't high by now, it won't take him long," I assure him before placing a quick kiss on his lips. "You just sit tight, and I'll be right back," I say, wanting to lighten the mood, but I see him struggle against his bonds like he's trying to stop me.

"Don't you dare, Harlow," he hisses as I step away and move to the steps. "Come back here. Harlow, if you do this, I swear I'm going to put you over my lap and spank you when I get out of here. There is a paddling bench with your name on it."

"Can't wait, babe," I tell him, blowing him a kiss, and I watch as he slumps, defeated in his chair.

"Be careful, please," he begs.

I make my way up the steps, my shoes quiet on them. When I get to the top, I slowly turn the handle and crack the door open. The noise of a party somewhere in the house reaches my ear, so I push the door open enough to peer around it. The door opens into a hallway with a couple more closed doors located along it. To the left are the sounds of the party, and the right looks to lead to a living area and the front door. If I were on my own, I would beeline toward that door, but I won't leave Jaxon behind, so I slowly head toward the closed door on the right. I want to avoid the party, and I'm hoping it might be a storage closet or a bedroom where I can find something to break the lock on the shackle.

Not being able to see the other side makes me nervous. I put my ear to the door in the hope that I can hear something, but it's an older-style house. The door is solid wood, so no noise is sneaking through. I'm not sure if it's empty or not, so I'm just going to have to take the risk.

Again, I slowly turn the handle then push the door open. There's a faint light, like a lamp is on, but before I can open it more, a noise down the hallway draws my attention. Fuck, someone is coming. Pushing the door open, I slip into the room and duck down low in case someone is in here.

My heart is racing, and I'm trying not to breathe too heavily when another noise catches my attention. My stomach sinks. Lifting my head, I look around. I've found a bedroom, and it isn't unoccupied. But thankfully, the occupants are too busy to notice me. My eyes widen as I take in the scene. On the bed is Cecelia, naked and hogtied with a ball gag in her mouth. Behind her, a greasy-looking old man is making piggy sounds as he fucks her ass.

"Take my big fat cock, you stuck-up bitch." He grunts and slaps her ass. "Your parents think they're so much better than the rest of us, but they still haven't been able to produce Bucătaru's little black book. I bet they don't even have it, or it doesn't even exist."

He continues his thrusting, and when Cecelia turns her head, I get a look at her face. Her eyes are squeezed tight, and there are tears streaming down her face. I almost feel sorry for her, but then I remember where I am. I might not have gotten my wish about her being fucked by a cactus , but she doesn't seem to be enjoying this either, so I'm pretty happy.

And now I know what Peter and Julia want, which fills me with an optimistic shot of triumph.

But I'm kind of stuck. If I go back out, I run the risk of running into someone in the hallway. I should probably hide under the bed or in the closet until they finish, but I have no desire to listen to this. So, as he reaches and wraps his hands around Cecelia's throat, thoroughly distracted, I creep back out of the room, praying there's no one on the other side of the door.

My luck sticks, and the breath I was holding whooshes out of me in relief. What I need to do is find the kitchen. Hopefully, there's an attached garage or carport with tools in there. So I go left toward the party, hoping that it's out the back of the house and not inside it. I don't get very far before another door down the hallway opens and a man stumbles out of it, tucking his dick back into his pants, followed by Raquel. She's wiping her mouth with the back of her hand. Two guesses what they were doing. The man sees me and smiles.

"Oh, I didn't realize there was a blonde option, too. I'll have a go at that one as well." Raquel frowns, not having noticed me yet, but when she does, her eyes widen as she shrieks.

"How did you get out? Mom!" she screams, running back down the hallway.

Fuck. I hurry back down to the basement, and Jaxon's eyes widen when he sees me taking the stairs two at a time. I look around the room for a weapon, eventually picking up Jacinta's chair. I'll just bash them over the head with it.

"I got caught, but on the bright side, maybe I'll get to kick Raquel's ass." We both watch the stairs, waiting with dread to see what will happen once they realize Jacinta is gone.

Chapter Twelve

Oliver

The room is chaos as everyone tries to talk over one another. Thomas is shouting into his phone while Kai and Holden throw questions at Dad, who obviously doesn't have any answers, but it's Declan's response that I'm most concerned about. He's gone quiet, and his eyes are glazed like he's retreated into his mind. What the fuck is wrong with my brave, self-assured, and arrogant-as-fuck big brother?

Ignoring everyone else, I move over to sit next to him. I pick his hand up in mine and pat it, trying to get his attention. "Dec… Dec." He doesn't respond. "Declan!" I call sharply, and that finally seems to work. His eyes meet mine, and although they're no longer blank, it's not much of an improvement. Instead, they're filled with terror.

Oh no, I guess this reminds him a little of when he lost his parents. He was with the neighbors while his mom and dad went out for date night, and when the police knocked on their neighbors' door later that evening, he was told they'd been in a car accident. A drunk driver had crossed over lanes and hit their car head-on. They'd been killed instantly. Child services had picked him up shortly after that because he had no family. Nana had told us that until the twins had come into his life, he'd been a withdrawn and quiet child, but once he took the two younger children under his wing, he changed. Being a big brother and having someone to look after gave him the purpose in life that he'd been missing since his parents' deaths. For the two of them to be missing, as well as Harlow, must have taken him back to that day so many years ago when he felt helpless and blamed himself.

"Get it together, man," I order, shaking him. "You're not helping anyone by becoming panicked. Let's not think the worst until we know something that gives us reason to." He blinks owlishly at me, but I can see him coming back on line. His back straightens, and he takes a deep breath before nodding at me.

"Thanks."

Thomas gets off the phone and roughly runs his fingers through his hair. "Jake is going to track the limo. I put devices on all the cars. I'm going down to security to look at the footage of their departure that night. It has to have happened between here and the cruise ship, so I'm guessing the usual driver had either been paid off or replaced. The guy's not answering any calls or texts, so either way, that doesn't bode well for him—or us. Jake's still coming up empty on Cecelia. It looks like she may have used a fake name and ID when we hired her. As soon as I'm done with the footage, I'm meeting Jake at her apartment. He has a warrant, and we're going to search it to see if we can find anything that points to her real identity or where she may be now."

"I don't understand why the stalker took the twins as well," Kai mutters.

"Maybe it was the only chance they got," Holden suggests. "Plus, it's not like either of the twins would let Harlow go without a fight. Maybe they were forced to take them all to make an easier getaway?" He has a pretty good point, but my mind has been nagging at this exact thought, and I've come up with an idea.

"What if it's all connected? If the remaining stalker has been watching Harlow this whole time, they've been learning about us too, right?" Everyone stares at me like they have no clue what I'm talking about.

"But what does that have to do with Cecelia?" Declan asks from next to me, his game face back on. I pat his knee reassuringly.

"What if Luke approached her? With the way she

treated Harlow and the rest of us, she blew her shot at staying a part of Neighpalm—threat of blackmail or not. Maybe Luke figured she could help him get Harlow for himself since Cecelia obviously wanted her out of the way, *and* if she had an ax to grind with the rest of us, he'd have a partner in getting some kind of revenge on us? He wanted Harlow, and she wanted to leech off of us. So long as they could both get what they wanted, does it really seem that far-fetched that they could have teamed up?" The more I think about it, the more it seems to make sense.

Declan shifts in his seat, drawing my attention back to him. "But we can't forget there's another person in play here, someone who obviously doesn't care whether Harlow is alive or not. This has got to be about their inheritance and the vault next door now, not just her. Someone wants something from that house, whether it's Cecelia or whoever else was working with or against Luke. We already assumed there were two people watching Harlow, and with Luke gone, that still leaves a mystery puppeteer in the background.""

"Well, who would benefit from Harlow being dead?" Holden asks, and the room falls quiet as we all rack our brains.

"I can't think of anyone. They didn't even know all of this when they were in Hawaii. The count's house hadn't been moved to her name yet since the twins were still dealing with the legalities of getting it moved to theirs first. And the money I gave her to start the animal sanctuary is in the business' name. We would all be devastated, of course, but unless their aim was just to hurt us, there is no direct benefit to killing Harlow." Dad's face shows strain, and we can all hear the tightness of his voice. He, like the rest of us, is hoping these theories are just that—hypothetical explanations that won't have any kernel of truth to them.

"Okay," Thomas says, a determined set to his mouth. "So we're at the point where we've got a lot of theories—the Bucătaru fortune might now be in play, Cecelia has hooked up with whoever was stalking Harlow alongside Luke, the twins were a lucky grab while Harlow was the main goal, or maybe even the opposite of that, depending on who's leading the show… Right now, we don't have any loose ends to explore as far as Harlow is concerned. We've checked out everyone we can on her end, but what about the twins? Did we ever get a lead on Carmen?"

"No, after the home invasion she disappears off the radar. She could be living it up in Bora Bora without a care in the world."

"Fuck, and now we're at a dead end again," Thomas grumbles.

"What can we do?" Dad asks, and Thomas shakes his head.

"Nothing at the moment unless you can think

of anything else that might be relevant. Did Carmen have any family besides the twins?"

"None she was close to as far as I knew." Dad breaks off, and a small frown appears between his eyebrows. "Before I went out to Connecticut to visit Chuck, Dragos and Carmen came to the house for dinner. They were supposed to be coming with me, but they pulled out at the last minute, said something had come up with his father." Dad runs a hand across his jaw. "It was weird because when they said goodbye, it felt like they were saying goodbye for good."

Dad's frown turns to a look of realization, and he jumps to his feet. "Holy shit! Carmen may be a dead end, but their father might not be. I'd forgotten all about this. As they were leaving, Dragos pulled this little black book out of his back pocket and gave it to me. We joked that it was his book of hookups and he was passing on the mantle because he had Carmen. But as he left, he told me to put it somewhere safe, said that I would know when the time was right to use it. I just laughed and shoved it in the top drawer of my office desk. By the time I got back from Connecticut, he was gone. I was so jaded about women I almost threw it in the trash, but out of respect for his last wish, I shoved it into my bookcase. It's been there ever since. If the twins really are connected to this somehow, it couldn't have started with them. It has to be connected to their father or grandfather. What if the book has some kind of clue?"

"We should definitely go have a look at what it says. You really never opened it?" Tom asks.

"No, never, I wasn't interested then, and once I started adopting all of you, I just felt too busy for any kind of romantic entanglements."

Next to me, Declan gets to his feet, and I can see he's finally back to normal because he starts throwing orders around. "Okay, Tom, you do whatever it is you need to do with Jake. The rest of us will go back to the house, and Dad will look for the book. Then I think we need to board up the access tunnels so that no one can get through them even if they have the security codes. With no locks on the outer entrances to the tunnels, that's our best shot of keeping anyone from getting in where they don't belong, and if we make it hard for them, that could provide enough time for us to catch someone trying to break in."

"We need to fix that once we get the twins and Harlow back," I point out as there's no doubt in my mind that we will get them back.

"Yeah, you're not wrong. Now that the police know they're there, that's far too many people in on the secret. Who knows if they have loose lips. Better to close them up and put keypads on them for more security." Like me, Kai seems outwardly calm. I know that he's feeling what I am—certainty that we will have Harlow back in our arms soon.

Tom's phone rings again as we're preparing to leave. "Hello? What?" His tone changes, drawing all of our attention. "Where? Okay. We'll get the chopper warmed up, and we'll be there as soon as we can. Are you sure? I don't know how comfortable I am with that. Sorry, you know I trust you. I just hate feeling useless. Make sure you're beside her for every word." There's another minute or two of silence before he sighs, his shoulders slumping. "Yup, thanks, man."

There's a grim frown on his face when he looks at us. "Jacinta just stumbled into a police station about twenty minutes from home. Thanks to the APB's Jake put on all of them, he was immediately notified once they learned who she was. Officers are going to take her statement. Jake is already on his way there, and he'll bring her home when they are done."

Kai's already grabbing his backpack and pulling out the keys to the chopper. "I'll have it ready to go in ten minutes," he tells us before racing out the door and up to the roof. "Well, don't just stand there. Get ready!" Dad shouts at us all.

Everyone finishes dressing and grabbing essentials, and before ten minutes are done, we're in the elevator on the way to the roof, Thomas included. With Jacinta coming back home to us, it's more important to hear what she might have to say before he goes racing off to Cecelia's.

The rotor blades are spinning at top speed as

the elevator doors open in front of us, and we hurry toward the helicopter. Within minutes, I feel the helicopter shudder as it takes off, then we're winging our way home. I'm just hoping she's okay and has some good news for us.

It's still super early in the morning when the helicopter lands at Dad's place. The family doesn't wait any longer than it takes for the helicopter to touch down before we're all climbing out. Poor Kai gets left behind to power down the machine while the rest of us race for the house, where Poppy meets us on the patio. "What's going on? Have you heard anything about the twins and Harlow? None of the hospitals in the area had anyone matching their descriptions." Poppy looks like he's aged ten years overnight. I've never seen him this distraught. We've been through some tough times, especially when each of us was adjusting to the family and relearning how to feel safe, but this is a whole new magnitude of trauma. I'm not sure any of us will let Jacinta or Harlow out of our sight for the foreseeable future.

"Yes," Dad says, not stopping, and we follow him into the house.

"Dad!" When he turns, a frown on his face, I nod at Poppy, then to Nana, who's sitting on the couch, weeping. Ben's arm around her, comforting her.

"Oh shit, sorry." Dad sighs and comes back to us, hugging his dad before sitting on the other side of his mom.

"Tell them what's happening, and that will give Kai a chance to catch up," Dad orders Thomas.

Nana starts weeping harder as he explains that Jacinta has been found, but we don't know what condition she's in or anything about the other two.

"Well, what are we waiting for? Let's go." Poppy leads the charge this time, but I'm the voice of reason, which is still sort of odd in itself. It's not like I don't have a good head on my shoulders, but I'm just so used to Tom or Dec being the boss when Dad's not filling that role.

"Hang on, let's just take a minute to gather ourselves. Dad, did you even tell Molly and Emma where you were going and why? Are they going to be worried? We also need to let Chuck and Melinda know what's going on. They don't even know that Harlow's missing!"

Everyone starts to talk, and Ben untangles himself from Nana. "Maybe I should go." A laugh almost bursts from my lips when he jumps at the resounding no that comes from my family.

"No, Ben, please stay… that's if you don't mind all the drama." With Poppy's request, Ben quickly places his butt back down on the couch with Nana.

"No, not at all. I'm happy to stay here. I just didn't want you to feel like I was intruding."

"How about we get Mrs. H out of bed to rustle us up some breakfast? We can make those calls to Chuck and Melinda and Molly and Emma, and by then I'm sure Thomas can get an update on how much longer we have to wait for Jazzy to get home," I suggest, and Ben shakes his head.

"No, don't wake your housekeeper. At least I can make myself useful," he says as he gets to his feet once more.

"Ben is a chef. He owns a chain of restaurants in Savannah," Nana tells us all as Holden smiles and shows Ben the way to the kitchen.

Dad pulls out his cell and calls his girlfriends, letting them know he'll send a car to bring them home. While he does that, Poppy calls Chuck and Melinda. By the time Kai makes it into the house, Dad's finished, and Poppy has reassurances that Chuck and Melinda are on their way.

My brother's puffing when he gets here but breathes a sigh of relief when he sees us.

"I thought for sure you would have been gone already," he says, grabbing a seat on the sectional.

"No, this one was the voice of reason for a change," Declan says dryly, pointing to me.

"You just be quiet. How about you call Max and let her know? I'm sure Chuck and Melinda are in such a panic they won't think about it." While Dec stares at me, a brow raised, I turn to my boyfriend. "And you should call Hope. Not only is she a member of the family, but this could be important for her to be aware of from a company standpoint, too. We need to get the PR team working on this as soon as possible for when the press catches wind of it. Now that Hope is taking over more at Neighpalm Records, we need someone else to take over what she usually takes care of. That's to figure out at another time, obviously, but right now, we need her to be informed. Plus, you know how quickly she's taken to Harlow. She'd kill us if we left her out of the loop on something happening to her new sister."

"Good thinking," Declan says, pulling out his phone.

"You won't reach her," Thomas quietly tells Declan, and I raise an eyebrow as he pulls us to the side. "Maxine asked me if she could use a plane and one of our holiday houses overseas. She needed a break, so I gave her the code to my place in Ireland. She should be there already since she was planning to leave yesterday morning."

"Without telling anyone? She made plans to have lunch with Harlow and Melinda and Chuck later this week. What's going on in her head?" I try to stare my brother down, but he just holds up his hands.

"She didn't tell me, but she looks tired and says she's been unwell and just needs a rest. I didn't want to pry because I hate it when people do that to me.

It's why I bought that property in Ireland in the first place."

Before I can respond, the doorbell rings.

"I'll get it." Declan leaves us, striding down the hallway, and we all patiently wait to see who it is.

Chapter Thirteen

Harlow

I stand there, chair raised over my head, my heart trying to beat out of my chest, my breath loud in my ear, waiting for someone to come down the stairs. I know it's only a matter of time.

"Harlow, don't be stupid! Get out of here. Save yourself. I'll be alright." Jaxon is shouting at me now, seeing no point in being quiet since we've already been made.

"Oh, don't be a martyr. We're in this together, Jax. You know, like 'til death do us part." He groans, tugging at the shackles, but all he succeeds in doing is digging them into his skin. He's going to have big bruises there if he's not careful.

"That's what I'm worried about," he mumbles, and there's this frustrated bitterness in his voice that makes my heart race for a different reason. He's worried about us—about me—and right now, I need him to be positive. We *can* get through this.

The door at the top of the stairs slams open, then feet rush down it. As they appear in my vision, I swing like I'm playing for the Yankees, and it's with great satisfaction that my chair collides with Raquel. She screams as her nose shatters, and blood starts pouring out as she tumbles the rest of the way down the stairs. I've pulled back the chair, readying myself to strike again, when Peter's voice stops me.

"Harlow, I have my gun aimed at Jaxon's head. If you even so much as twitch, I'll put a bullet through his brain. We'll simply go back to plan A and ransom you."

I drop the chair to the floor, ignoring Raquel rolling around in pain, and move in front of Jaxon, hopefully taking his death off the table.

"Don't you dare put yourself between me and that gun!" he screams at me and rattles his restraints even more as Peter emerges.

"How the fuck did you get out of that chair?" he asks as Julia steps down behind him. Before I can answer, Julia's gasp alerts me to the fact that she's noticed they're missing a key player.

"Where is she? Where's Jacinta?" She tries to launch herself at me, but Peter holds her back.

"Well, that is a shame. I guess our timeline just got pushed up. The two of you are going to follow every one of my instructions, or I won't hesitate to start putting bullets in you. I won't kill you instantly, so don't make the foolish assumption that you'll be saving yourself any pain. It will be gut shots, and the one who isn't shot will have to listen as the other slowly bleeds to death. Get the keys out of my pocket, Julia, and release Jaxon. We're going to have to take a trip."

He nudges Raquel with his shoe. "Get up and stop your wailing, you annoying bitch. Grab those ropes and tie Harlow's hands together. Then go fetch your sister."

Raquel staggers to her feet, and I feel immense satisfaction at the sight of her swollen face. It looks like I may have knocked out a tooth, too. Score one for me. That will teach her to put her filthy hands on what's mine.

"Cecelia is busy entertaining Sergio," Julia tells Peter, and he cackles.

"In that case, she's going to be useless to us. Dammit. Fine, it will have to be just the three of us. We need to hurry and get out of here. I'm sure the police will be on their way soon."

Raquel staggers over to me, grabbing the rope that came off Jacinta from the floor. "Hands behind your back, Harlow, or Jaxon gets the first bullet. All we need is one drop of blood."

"You need the code, too." I sneer back at him as I hold my hands out to Raquel. She ties the rope around them none too gently as Julia releases Jaxon from his shackles before tying rope around his wrists as well. I see him wince in pain now that he's rubbed them raw from struggling against his restraints.

"I bet Jaxon sings like a canary the moment I threaten to put a bullet in you. I'm not worried, Harlow, though I think you should be." Peter is smiling maniacally, and I don't doubt he'll do as he says.

"Let's go." He gestures up the stairs with his gun, and both Jaxon and I start walking up them. "Don't even think about making a run for it," he warns, and I see Jaxon's shoulders sag like he's lost hope. But I refuse to go out like this. My life was shit because of this woman fucking with it. Anger surges through me at the thought of what it could have been if she and her manipulative, narcissistic tendencies had left my mom alone. A small feeling of sadness rolls over me, but I've made peace with my life and only want to look forward. I will *not* let her wreck mine like she did Mom's, so the first moment I get, I'm fighting back.

The trunk of their car is cramped with Jaxon and I squeezed in together. There's not even enough room for us to help each other undo our ropes. Not that it would do us any good. We're traveling too fast to throw ourselves out the back.

By the time we've been driving for what has to be at least thirty minutes, my limbs are tingling from lack of circulation. I'm trying to wriggle into a position where I can try to untie his hands, but Jaxon lets out a pained groan that makes me freeze.

"Fuck, babe, I'm sorry. I didn't mean to hurt you." I lean forward and brush my lips against his, not wanting to split it again by putting too much pressure on it.

He starts to chuckle. "I wasn't groaning because of my ribs. I was groaning because you're rubbing against my body, and it feels good." I blink a couple of times and shake my head.

"I cannot believe you can get hard in a time like this," I lightly scold him, and I feel his lips turn up.

"But you're fucking sexy, and I love you."

"I know, and I love you too. I plan on showing you many times, but let's get out of here first. If you're a good boy, I'll let you have full rein of the sex room. I'll be nothing but your fuck toy."

He takes my mouth with his, ignoring the cut, and kisses me with desperate fury. A taste of copper hits my tongue as it tangles with his, and I know his lip has started bleeding again. Panting, I pull away. "Babe, focus."

Before he can say anything, the car starts to slow down. The drive starts to get bumpier, and Jaxon and I are tossed around in the trunk. My head bangs against something sharp. "Ow, fuck, that hurt," I mutter, then I feel something trickle down my face. Shit, I must be bleeding.

"Are you okay?" Jaxon asks as we continue to jostle around.

""No, I think I cut myself. Where do you think we are?"

"I bet we're going down that service track that runs down the side of the house."

"Dad's?" I ask him, confused.

"No, ours," he tells me, and my heart melts despite the circumstances. I love hearing him call it ours.

"They talked about taking us to the vaults, and we have to go through the tunnels because neither of us have the keys. Thank god I gave them to Oli and Holden the night of the gala."

"How long do you think they've had us?" The car hits a particularly nasty bump, and I throw myself on top of Jaxon in the hope that I don't cut my head again.

He grunts beneath the sudden pressure of my weight. "They grabbed us from the gala, but I think this is the next evening, so the family probably hasn't noticed we're even missing. Though hopefully Thomas will soon, if he hasn't already. His level of paranoia can be extreme,."

My heart sinks at his words. "No, they probably haven't. Hopefully Jacinta makes it somewhere so she can call for help, or Thomas puts two and two together."

"Who knows how long we've been driving? It might take her a while to find help," Jaxon reminds me, and I feel even more depressed.

Finally, the car rolls to a stop, and within minutes, the trunk is opening. Peter is standing there, holding a pistol at our faces, the second that I have a clear view of what awaits us. Behind him, I can see the sky lighting up, so the sun must be starting to rise. It'd almost be a pretty sight if it wasn't interrupted by Raquel and Julia's looming figures, guns now clenched in their hands, too.

"Get moving," Peter orders, but it's not like he offers to help, so with great difficulty, we struggle our way out of the car. When I look around, I realize Jaxon was right. We're at the beginning of the zoo, so now we need to trek through it to get to the tunnels. Unfortunately, we're too early for there to be any workmen on site. I was hoping one of the McCallister brothers would be here, but they'd probably just end up getting shot.

"You're never going to get away with this," Jaxon promises them as Peter gestures for us to start moving. "Workmen will be on site today, and they're going to wonder whose car that is."

"Well, I suggest you hurry up if you want to save their lives," Peter snarls.

"Maybe we should wait until tonight," Julia says from behind us before there's a smacking sound. She cries out in pain, the sound giving me a slight flicker of satisfaction that I in no way feel guilty about.

"No. Because of your stupid bitch daughters, the other one got free. How long do you think it will take for them to figure out we're in the tunnels? We need to do this quickly." Jaxon and I had deliberately slowed down as they argued, but he suddenly stumbles forward when Peter shoves him from behind. "Get moving. Don't fuck with me."

"What is it you want?" I ask, not wanting to lay all my cards on the table. He has no idea what I did or didn't overhear, and I'd like it to stay that way for now. "Maybe if you told us, we would be able to find it quickly for you."

"No," he snaps.

"Peter, it might not hurt. They may know where it is, then we can be done with this," Julia cajoles.

There's silence for a moment as we trudge our way through the zoo, but a noise up ahead has me stopping. The sound of hooves on the uneven footpath. Slowly, I move to the side of the path, my eyes imploring Jaxon to follow me, and he quickly does the same.

Peter finally notices our movement. "Hey, what are you doing?" he yells, loud enough to scare the herd of deer that's just out of sight. And as I had hoped instead of running away from us the stupid creatures run toward us, coming around the corner in a mad out of control dash.

Our kidnappers shout with surprise and try to

move out of the way, but they're not quick enough. As they get battered by the panicked animals, I shove Jaxon.

"Go! Maybe we can lose them in the zoo."

He and I move as well as we can with our hands tied, though at least I have a slight advantage over everyone else because I actually know where I'm going. If we can make it to the tiger's cage and down to the tunnel before the other three, we can lock them out by closing the door on the vault end of the tunnel.

But we've still got to make it there first, and there's about a hundred yards to go. It's still not completely light out, and we can't go as fast as I'd like on the uneven surface.

"Fuck!" I hear Peter shout behind us. "If you don't stop now, I *will* put a bullet in Raquel. Do you want to be responsible for her death?" I slow down, and Jaxon runs into me.

"What are you doing?" he hisses, and my shoulders sag.

"I don't really want her death on my conscience. After everything they've put us through feeling guilt from her death would be horrible. "

"She wants to rape me!" he argues, but I shake my head.

"I know she's an evil bitch, but she's my cousin, Jax. Lets look at it this way. She wasn't lucky enough to have Melinda, Chuck or a Brad in her life to save her. We'd probably be a lot like her and Cecelia if we didn't either."

His eyes soften, and his shoulders slump as he sighs. "Fuck, you're right. I wish you weren't, but you are."

We stop, and I call back, "We're not running anymore. Don't hurt her."

The three of them walk around the corner, with Raquel propped up between Julia and Peter. She looks like she might be unconscious.

"I said dont hurt her," I spit at him, and he starts to chuckle like the evil bastard he is.

"I didn't. Stupid bitch wasn't fast enough, so she got trampled by the deer." Just then, she starts to groan, regaining consciousness. Peter drops her arm, and Julia sags with Raquel's weight held against her. For a moment, I thought she might complain, but all she does is slap Raquel hard across the face.

"Wake up! You're useless. We should have brought your sister. At least she's good for more than spreading her legs."

What a nasty bitch.

Raquel's eyes flutter open, and I watch her struggle to stand on her own while Peter shakes his head. "Just leave her. We need to keep moving."

Surprisingly, Julia chooses that moment to act like a mother. "No, she's not safe here. What if the workmen arrive early?"

"I don't care. We need to be quick. We'll pick her up on the way back."

Julia leads her over to the wall of a nearby enclosure and helps her sit down. "When you can, go back to the car and wait for us there," she instructs her daughter who still looks dazed but seems to understand.

"Right, let's go get my little black book then, shall we?" Peter says as Julia straightens up, and they both wave their guns to get us moving.

Chapter Fourteen

Holden

W hen I return from showing Ben the kitchen and everything he needs, the family is looking down the hallway, and Declan is missing.

"Where's Dec?" I whisper in Oli's ear as I wrap my arm around his waist, offering him some much needed comfort. The both of us are wired tight, and I can't say I'm not taking comfort in it as well as he leans into me.

"The doorbell rang, so he went to answer it," he whispers back, not taking his eyes off the hallway.

A shout at the front door has everyone else jumping to their feet. Thomas holds out his hand to stop us from running out the front right before he does just that. It's not long before he returns, followed by Jake, his spy buddy, and Declan with his arm wrapped around our sister.

"Jazzy!" Nana cries out, bursting into tears, while the rest of us surround her, passing her around for hugs. When she gets in my arms, I hold her tight. She's sobbing, and everyone keeps throwing questions at her.

"Hey, just slow down!" Jake shouts above all the noise. "Give her some space and let her tell the story. It needs to be quick because we've got to get moving."

I help her into the seat on the other side of Nana, who grabs her hand and holds it tight while Jacinta takes a deep breath. Now that I can look at her, I realize her face is swollen, and there's a scab on her lip from where it's been bleeding. Her hair is a mess, and she looks exhausted.

Ben bustles out with a cup of coffee and a bottle of water. "I heard the commotion. Here, get something warm into you. It might help with the shock." He hands the coffee to my sister and passes the bottle of water to Nana, who smiles gratefully at him, before he returns to the kitchen.

Jacinta hip nudges Nana with a small smile on her face. "So is this a thing now?" she asks as she takes a sip of the hot coffee and then sighs.

Nana shushes her. "Stop it. Tell us everything."

Jacinta proceeds to tell us a story that blows our minds. It's just twisted enough that even though we might have found some kernels of truth, there was no fucking way we ever could have figured all of this out. When she gets to the part about Julia's role in breaking up Dad and Diane, the look on his face is heartbreaking. A tear trickles down his face, and I let go of Oli to comfort Dad instead.

"Hey, Dad, come sit down." Most of us stayed standing when Jazzy came in, so I encourage him to take a seat on the other side of her. He grabs the hand not currently holding her coffee and squeezes it.

Eventually, she runs out of words and slumps against the couch, exhausted, then Jake takes over.

"When Jacinta stumbled into the police station early this morning, I was immediately alerted. She was able to tell us how to get back to the place where they were all held. We're hoping they haven't noticed she's missing yet since they were having some kind of party when she got free."

"That seems like a long shot to me," Kai grumbles, and Jake shoots him a sympathetic look.

"Yeah, it's not a lot to go on, but it's our only lead at the moment."

"I'm coming with you. Give me five minutes," Thomas orders as he hurries down the hallway to get changed, I guess.

Again, we hear a commotion at the front door, but when I go to see what's happening, Melinda and Chuck come rushing down the hallway. When she sees Jazzy, Melinda cries out, her eyes darting around like she's trying to find Harlow as well. The moment she realizes Harlow isn't here, she bursts into tears.

Dad gets up and goes over to the two of them. "Come sit, I'll fill you in on what's happening. We have to let Jake and Thomas go."

Melinda follows Dad, but Chuck has a familiar stubborn set to his shoulders. He crosses his arms. "No way, I want to go wherever they are," he insists, but Melinda cries even louder, shaking her head, and he visibly softens. "Okay, I'll stay and wait. I trust you guys to get our Harlow."

"We aren't going to take no for an answer," Oli chimes in, turning to look at Jake. I know that Jake is going to have a major argument on his hands if he says no, so I'm relieved when he nods.

"I thought you might say that. You can come, but you have to stay back until either Thomas or I give you the all-clear. That is non-negotiable. I will *not* have civilians getting in the way."

"Agreed," Oli immediately says, looking mighty pleased with himself.

"Dad, you, Chuck, and Poppy stay here. We'll let you know as soon as we find them," Declan says as Thomas returns wearing his bulletproof vest over the top of his shirt. He already has his gun in hand, checking the magazine.

"Let's go," Jake says, and the five of us follow him out. When we reach the foyer, Thomas turns to us. "Declan, you come with me and Jake. You three go in my SUV."

Kai, Oli, and I head toward the garage exit while Declan follows Thomas and Jake out the front, and soon enough, we're flying down the driveway.

"I can't believe Raquel is involved with this as well. I hope we can get to them before she tries to do anything to Jaxon. What's with the Summer boys attracting batshit crazy women?" Oli's low ramble shifts the back of my mind, my focus on the way we're speeding down the road.

"Like you haven't dated your fair share of freaks. What about that guy in college who wouldn't go out on a full moon? It wasn't until the third month that you discovered it was because he thought he was a werewolf because he insisted you chain him to the bed so he wouldn't infect you. Jacinta didn't let you live that down for months," Kai snaps back, going on the defense, and I cringe as I remember who he's talking about. Oliver was with that guy for about three months, and I avoided going anywhere I thought they might be during that time. It was awful.

"Yeah, yeah, baby daddy," Oli mutters defensively, and I hush him.

"Stop it now, both of you. No point in tearing into one another. We've got to be team Summers to help Jaxon and Harlow through this," I scold them, desperately hoping there's a Jaxon and Harlow to get through this once we're done.

The wait in the car is excruciating. Declan joined us once we arrived, and our car was parked out of the way of the house that the others had been kept in. It was about a half-hour drive from our place, sitting at the end of a long dirt drive, almost surrounded by trees. We're under strict directions not to come down until we get a call from our brother or Jake.

By the time we get the all-clear, we're all ready to run to the house if needed. Kai rushes our car down the driveway instead, and the four of us jump out once we pull up next to Jake's car. There's a lot of police officers milling around, and an uneasy feeling washes over me as I scan the chaos for a hint of my brother or our girlfriend. Thomas' face confirms what I'm afraid of when he comes slamming out the front door of the house.

"Fuck!" he screams, and my heart sinks. No, they can't be dead. I grab for Oli's hand, and he latches onto me, expressing my thoughts out loud.

Our brother comes striding over to us, and with each step, his face settles into something that's closer to anger than devastation. Maybe the worst hasn't happened yet?

"They're not here," he tells us when he gets to us, and although I'm disappointed, I'm also relieved that he's not giving us worse news. "They must have moved after they realized Jacinta was missing." Just as he says that, Jake leads a man out, handcuffed, and starts reading him his rights.

"Who's that?" Declan asks, nodding at the dude, and Thomas sighs heavily. Before he can answer, more men are led out as well as a couple of women.

"All of them were passed out inside the house. I'm assuming this is the party that Jacinta said they were having. The women are whores and one of them was happy to tell us everything. Apparently, she was close enough to the head guy that she knew some details of his plans. The guy with Jake is Sergio Garcia. He's high up in the chain of the Carrera Cartel out of Mexico, and he was a known associate of the count many years ago. We think the two of them may have had a sex trafficking ring going on. The details the woman shared about what their *clients* like to do... Well, they cater to men who have some depraved tastes."

"Like what?" Oli asks, and I cringe, waiting for the answer.

"They like to kill and torture while they fuck," Thomas says flatly. "There's something else," he adds, and there's a small hint of something that might be satisfaction in his eyes when he looks between us and the house again. "Cecelia won't be a problem anymore. It's safe to say that she won't be sabotaging anyone ever again."

"She's dead?" Declan asks, sounding shocked, and Thomas nods. Declan heads to the house like he wants to make sure for himself, but none of us follow him. Thomas doesn't even try to stop him.

"Yeah, it's not pretty. She's got bruises around her throat, and she'd been sexually assaulted—both anally and vaginally—with a knife."

"Her mother left her to die?"

Thomas shrugs, looking much less fazed than Kai and his incredulous question. "Sergio is well known for his proclivities. She must have had an idea what might happen if she let him play with her daughter."

I feel ill, and I can see that my other brothers do too. Cecelia wasn't a nice person, but no one deserves *that*. Declan stumbles back out of the house, looking pale, and hurries over to a bush before we hear him retching into it. Despite our special privileges, what with Thomas being our brother, he still wouldn't have wanted to fuck up the crime scene by contaminating evidence.

"Fuck!" Kai whispers before going over to check on our big brother. We watch as he talks to him, too far away to make out what they're saying. Declan's wiping his mouth with the back of his hand, his face a little more alert, after a moment.

"I think there was a bottle of water in the car." Oli goes back to it to have a look as the other two head back to us. I don't ask what he saw. If he had that kind of reaction, I don't want to know.

Paramedics come out of the house, wheeling a stretcher with a sheet draped over it, the outline of a body underneath. Jake follows behind them, and when he sees us, he comes over.

"That whore just gave me some more information that you guys need to hear," Jake says, the breathless words rushing out. Thomas' body tightens in anticipation. When our brother turns back to us, there's a steely, focused glint in his eyes. Gone is the anger from what he found inside the house. This is Thomas on the job, and seeing that gives me a burst of hope.

"The whore told us that Peter made some kind of deal with Sergio—for information. He was supposedly selling him some little black book that had details on all his suppliers, clients, and the properties he used for *business* in it. We think the goal was to get into any other caches of guns and drugs before the authorities, or your family, found them. She said she overheard them saying they needed to get into the vault today."

"Holy shit! Could that be the book that Dad was talking about? But if they're going to the vault, they obviously don't know that Dragos gave it to Dad. If that's the right book, that is. Fuck! How do we know for sure?" Oli almost shouts the words, and I quickly shush him, but Jake and Thomas exchange a conspiratory glance.

"Well, what are we waiting for? Let's go!" Declan rushes back to our car, and we follow him as Thomas and Jake get in Jake's.

Within moments, we're heading back in the

opposite direction, the car quiet while we all soak in the information about Cecelia and the fact that we finally know what all this is about.

It's Oli that breaks the silence. He and I are sitting in the back, taking comfort from one another, when he gasps and sits bolt upright.

"What? What's wrong, babe?" I ask, looking around for what might have upset him.

"I think I might know where that book is if there's one in our house," he announces excitedly. "When Harlow and I were looking around that first day, we found a safe in the panic room. The same safe we found the map in, remember?"

"Yeah, I remember you telling us about it. You said it has some other things in it, but you didn't go into detail," Kai says, not taking his eyes off the road. A guilty look crosses Oli's face, but he smooths it over. I make a note to ask him about it when this is all over, but I don't want to distract him from wherever he's going with this now.

"One of the things we found was a little black book. I didn't actually open it at the time since I was more excited about the map, but what if that's what they're looking for?"

"So Harlow knows where this is?" Declan asks, turning to look back at the two of us, and Oli nods.

"Yeah, she does. Is that a good thing?" Declan turns back around, shrugging his shoulders.

"Maybe? Maybe she can buy them some time by not telling them an exact location, but if they threaten Jaxon in any way, she won't hesitate to tell them where it is."

"So if the little black book is in the vault in the panic room, what do you think the book Dad has is?" I remind them. The silence in the car is heavy as we all think about that.

Kai breaks the silence with a theory that makes my blood run cold. "What if it's like a two-part thing? What if one of them had the contacts, and the other person had the codes? Like a safe-keeping thing. If someone was so inclined to take the count's empire by force, they would need both books to have all the information. When Dragos decided to make a run for it with Carmen, what if he gave his half to Dad for safe-keeping?"

"And when they find the book and realize they only have half the information, it won't take them long to assume that Brad may have the other half. He's the only person alive who might have it if it's not at our place. It's not like the count had a reputation for trustworthy allies, and with Dragos' body missing, there's no proof to say that he didn't run off with information before he disappeared." Declan sounds grim.

"That's true... Dragos' body is still missing. Hopefully, Harlow is smart enough to tell them that. Maybe they'll assume he still has his half since neither Jaxon nor Harlow know Dad has it. Maybe that will keep them alive a little longer if they're in a tailspin, trying to figure out where to look next."

Even I can hear the doubt in my own voice, but how am I supposed to feel? This is all too unpredictable to really let myself hope.

"But what if they do know? Remember, Julia knew Carmen, who probably was told or at least assumed that Dragos would use Dad as a safe place. That was probably why she and her crew did the home invasion! What if she spilled the beans, and Dad's place is the next target?" Oli sounds frantic, and I dig out my phone at the same time Declan does.

"I'll call Dad, and you call Jake," I tell him, adrenaline making my hand shake as I try to find Dad's number. "I just hope we're not too late."

Chapter Fifteen

Harlow

I flinch as Peter and Julia shout at one another. They're tearing apart the vault while Jaxon and I stand off to the side. With the pallet of drugs and guns confiscated by the authorities, the front half is oddly empty, and their shrieking echoes around us.

"It's got to be here. It wasn't at the funeral parlor when I searched the clothing that was with the remains." Peter is growing more and more agitated with every minute that passes, which doesn't bode well for us. When will he start taking that frustration out on us? *Maybe I should just tell them what I know.* My eyes slide to Jaxon, and I can see that he's watching them, a thoughtful look on his face.

"What if Dragos found it and hid it some-where?" His words silence the arguing couple.

Julia sneers at him. "And where would he have taken it? To heaven when I killed him?"

"He's not dead." Jaxon's announcement stops them both in their tracks, and Julia scoffs.

"Of course he is! I killed him myself."

"We only found one body, and that was identi-fied as his father. If what you say is true, and you killed them both in here, where did Dragos' body go?"

She's shaking her head in denial, though at this point I'm not sure whether it's due to her actual belief or a tactic for survival. With the fury radi-ating off of Peter, she'd better pray she convinces him she didn't fuck up.

"No, I shot them both! They must have been in here."

Jaxon shrugs, playing it cool. "You may have shot them, but that doesn't mean you killed them. Dragos could still be alive. If you had the chance to disappear, wouldn't you take it?"

The sound of the gun shot is deafening. I watch in shock as a bullet hole blooms in the middle of Julia's forehead. In what feels like slow motion, my aunt's body tumbles to the ground, a small pool of blood gathering around her head.

"Useless fucking bitch." Peter snarls, then roots around in her pockets for her phone, shoving it in his before turning on us. "Well, if that's the case, I have no use for you. Looks like we're going back to ransoming you, Harlow." I know the next bullet is going between my lover's eyes if I don't do something. My mind races, trying to figure out my angle, then I remember something that they had talked about in the basement with Raquel. Fuck, I hope Jaxon has as much faith in me as I did in him.

"Wait, wait!" I shout, ignoring Jaxon's protests when I step in front of him. "I think I know where it is, what you're looking for. It's upstairs in the panic room safe."

The fury leaves his eyes, replaced with surprise. "There's a panic room?"

"Ah yeah, it's off of the secret sex room."

"Do you know the codes?" He's laser focused on me now that he knows I might have what he wants.

"I do, but I want a cut." He blinks at me in surprise, and I bring a sultry smile to my face and lower my voice so it's husky and sexy.

"Look, let's be real now that it's just you and me. I can't stand these pretty boys. They were just my ticket to what I really wanted. If I can get a cut of whatever it is that you're selling those books for, I won't have to keep spreading my legs for these assholes." I inwardly cross my fingers in the hope that I'm speaking his language. Men like Peter only see women as a commodity or a drain. Appealing to his inner misogynist may be enough to keep Jaxon and me alive for a little longer.

"I mean, I was hoping to get knocked up by this

one so that my baby would be the new heir to the Bucătaru fortune, but his bitch sister is still in the way. If I help you with this, and you help me with that, I'll split my stuff with you, too." I play my final card, hoping that it will seal the deal and keep us both alive.

I can see the wheels turning in Peter's head while I hold my breath. All of this is so fucked up. I cannot believe how messed up these people are. I swear if we get out of this alive, I'm going to make sure Chuck and Melinda know how grateful I am for them and their love. I shudder when I think of how easily I could have ended up like Raquel and Cecelia.

"I like how you think, Harlow. You've got a bit of your mom in you after all. She liked to spread her legs for cash too." He chuckles, and I cringe as I remember this guy was one of my mom's clients.

But then his smile drops. "But what do you have any need for him for? You've got access to all of Brad's fortune."

My mind races as I try to come up with a reason. "Yeah, but I have to split it eight ways, probably nine now that my fucking father has adopted another child. That much money doesn't go as far when that needs to happen. If my mother had been honest with him, there would be no splitting it. She fucked it up for me, made me suffer, and now I want what I'm due. If I can produce an heir to this fortune with no other family around, it, and by default *me*, will be the sole beneficiary. " I feel ill speaking those kinds of words out loud, but I can see that they really resonate with the vile man in front of me.

He considers my words carefully, and finally he nods. "Fine, but don't even think of double crossing me. You now know what happens to people who fuck things up for me." His eyes slide to the rapidly cooling body of my aunt, her blood pooling around her head. He waves his gun at the two of us. "Let's get moving. We're going to go upstairs and find that black book. If you give me the book, I'll support you in your bid to get pregnant with the heir. Then we'll kill off Jaxon, and Jacinta can have a mysterious accident."

I bite my lip with worry as I turn to walk out of the vault, pleading with my eyes for Jaxon to go along with this.

"But, Harlow…" I turn and look back at Peter. "As soon as I have that book, you *are* going to fuck. I will watch, and I'm not letting you out of my sight until I have you confirmed knocked up and Jaxon is dead. Don't fuck me over because I won't hesitate to kill you." He waves his gun at me, then points it at Jaxon who is still slightly behind me. "Then him, and then I'll kill the rest of your family. Actually, I might do it the other way so I can make you watch."

I want to vomit, but I swallow it down and saunter out of the vault. Or try to. Turning, I hold my hands out. "Untie me, and I'll call down the elevator."

He narrows his eyes with suspicion but leans forward and does as I've asked—one handed since he keeps the gun on Jaxon the whole time. I could try to fight him, but he wouldn't need to be accurate to actually hit Jax, so I bide my time.

I hurry to the elevator and put in the code, bringing it down to us. The sooner I can get him the black book, the better. There was also a gun in that safe, so I'm hoping he's distracted enough that I can get my hands on it and use it.

The elevator arrives, and the three of us step onto it, moving upward once I put in the code.

"So, Jaxon, how does it feel to be betrayed by yet another woman? First Raquel and now Harlow. You've really got to start questioning your taste in women. Maybe you should be like your fag brothers."

My fists clench at my side when he mentions Oli and Holden in such a derogatory way. I can't wait to get my hands on that gun.

Jaxon is quiet, but Peter doesn't like that. He pistol whips him across the face, and I can't stop the cry that leaves my mouth.

"Fuck, why did you do that? He's already messed up enough. How do you expect me to fuck him if you damage him?"

Jaxon spits blood onto the floor of the elevator. "Traitorous bitch! If I had my hands free, I would wrap them round your throat and strangle the life out of her." He sounds cold and furious, and when my eyes meet his in the mirror of the elevator walls, they're filled with hate. He's really selling the anger.

Peter cackles at Jaxon's hostility. "I like how you think, my friend. I also like to wrap my hands around a lady's throat and choke the life out of them. You could say it's my speciality."

The elevator doors open, and I step out and down the secret stairs. Jaxon and Peter follow behind me, the latter's eyes wide with surprise as he takes in his uncle's house.

"Holy shit, this is fucking fancy." He whistles as I lead him up the stairs to the next level and into the other secret elevator.

"My uncle was always a paranoid bastard. You know, he paid me to kill my parents and sisters. Told me he didn't want any competition for his wealth. I guess allowing me to live should have clued me in to the fact that he knew I had no claim on his fortune," Peter muses, more to himself than me or Jaxon, but he's still got the gun pointing at us. How is his arm not getting tired?

For the last time, the doors open, and we step out into the sex room. "Woo wee, look at this room. My uncle really was a kinky fuck." Peter sounds excited, and when he looks at me, his eyes are shining with lust. Holy fuck, is he getting ideas? He licks his lip and steps toward me.

"Oh hey, there are party favors in the safe up

here. Why don't we grab those? From the looks of Jaxon, I don't think there's any chance he'll fuck me willingly now that I've admitted the truth." I hurry away from him, beelining for the sex closet.

After a moment, Peter follows me in, his eyes widening when I pull out the brick of coke and a big bag of pills. He's practically licking his lips. Oh yeah, I recognize that look—junkie stare.

He slaps me on the ass. "Come on, then. Let's do this. We still need to grab the book and get out of here before anyone shows up for the day."

"It's still early. We have plenty of time," I tell him, hoping he'll be too distracted by the drugs to use his common sense. There was a clock on the wall on the landing near the second elevator, which showed it was about 6:30. Surely, construction crews start early, don't they? On the other hand, I don't think he would hesitate to shoot anyone we come across, so maybe I hope they don't start early.

When we go back, Jaxon is on the bed inside the cage and the door is locked behind him. Peter must have put him in there before he followed me into the closet. Peter places the brick of coke on one of the sex benches and unlocks the cage, holding the gun on Jaxon the whole time. "Get in here and put him in the shackles."

I hurry over to do as he asks, untying the rope around Jaxon's wrists before putting first one, then the other, into the shackles on either side of the bed. Peter stands over me the whole time. Fuck, I thought he would make us grab the book first. I can't believe I'm going to have to fuck Jaxon in front of him.

"I thought we were going for the book first?" I say, trying to stall.

"I was, but it would be a waste of such a perfectly good room if one of us doesn't get to use it. Unless you want me to fuck you." I quickly shake my head, and he grunts, "That's what I thought. Now, do his legs, but take off his pants first so they don't get in the way." I swallow the lump in my throat and climb onto the bed, crawling toward Jaxon with a plea in my eyes for him to understand, but he won't even look at me. I smother a sob that tries to escape and get to work on pulling down his suit pants.

Once I have them over his ankles, I put them on the floor. As I go back up to remove his briefs, a noise has me turning my head. Peter is bent over the paddling bench with a line of coke all ready to go. Next to the brick of coke lies his gun, a bank card, and a dollar bill. I watch as he rolls the dollar bill and snorts the white powder up, throwing his head back once he's done. Jesus, that was quick. I hadn't taken all that long to take Jaxon's pants off, but I must admit I'm dawdling more than I would if we were doing this for real. Peter turns to stare at me, eyes wide, looking more than slightly unhinged. Fuck, I think I just made it worse. Now he's high with an itchy trigger finger.

"Get on with it." He waves his hand at me before using the bank card to set up another line. I focus back on removing Jaxon's briefs. "I'm so sorry," I whisper to him while Peter is distracted. His jaw is tight like he's gritting his teeth, his whole body strung taut with anger.

His briefs join his pants on the floor, and I move his legs into the shackles at the end of the bed. I cannot believe this is happening. This was not what I had in mind when I used that excuse. Then something occurs to me, the last card I've got to play right now.

"I'm on the pill," I tell Peter. "This isn't going to work today. I need time to come off it."

He stops what he's doing and narrows his eyes at me. "It's been two days since you've been able to take it. I think we can risk it. Besides, if at first you don't succeed, then we'll just fucking try again."

"But look, Jaxon isn't even hard." I gesture to my boyfriend, praying I haven't completely ruined everything between us.

"How about I give him a little hit? That might help." Peter digs his finger into the brick of coke, and it comes out covered in the white powder, with a little pile sitting on the pad. Picking up the gun, he walks into the cage and aims it at me.

"Bite me, and I'll shoot her. It won't be a killing shot because I still need her, but it will be painful, and she will die slowly," he tells Jaxon who glares at him.

"Go ahead and shoot her. I don't care. I can't believe I let myself fall for another backstabbing whore. My family must be cursed," Jaxon spits out, his eyes trained on Peter.

He moves the gun and puts it at Jaxon's head instead. "Fine, I'll just shoot you." Thankfully, Jaxon's sense of self-preservation is bigger than his anger at me, so he holds still.

"Get naked," Peter tells me as he shoves his finger into Jaxon's mouth, rubbing the powder all over his gums before pulling back. "I'm sure that will help Jaxon. He's a redblooded man, and you're fucking hot. Flash him some titties and that gash, and the powder will do the rest."

Fuck. It looks like I'm not going to get out of this. Peter exits the cage and slams it shut behind him, locking us in before going back to his line of coke.

I start to peel off my shirt as I hear him snort up the drugs, my mind running through my options and finding no solutions. My heart sinks. I'm going to have to go through with this to keep us both alive.

Chapter Sixteen

Harlow

Peter wanders around, poking and prodding at the different apparatuses before he gets to the cabinet of sex toys. He whistles as he pulls it open. "Look at all these toys. You want anything from this cupboard over here, Harlow?" he calls back conversationally like he's not making us have sex at gunpoint.

He turns to look at me, but when he sees I'm still wearing my underwear, he frowns. "Tick tock, Harlow, we're a little pressed for time. Get naked and shake those titties in front of him." There's nothing I can do, so I climb onto the bed with the man I love and try to pretend Peter isn't in the room.

Reaching behind my back, I flick the clasp on

my bra and lean forward. It falls down my arms, and I toss it onto the floor with Jaxon's pants. When my eyes meet his, the anger is gone. His pupils are dilated so wide it looks like there's no color left in his eyes. I crawl until I'm straddling his body, hoping I can stop Peter from seeing most of what we're doing.

A goofy grin softens Jaxon's face as his gaze drops to my naked breasts. "God, I love your tits," he mumbles quietly, and I feel his cock start to harden underneath me. Looking around, Peter is nowhere to be seen. He must have stepped into the costume closet where I found the drugs, so I lean in and kiss Jaxon. His tongue tangles clumsily with mine, and as I pull away, he tries to follow, but his restraints hold him in place.

"I'm so sorry," I lean in and whisper in his ear. "Please tell me you didn't believe anything I said."

"Of course I didn't," he says just as quietly. "I couldn't look at you because you're so hot, and I couldn't control my dick at the thought of you and me making a baby together." His honesty has me sitting up, blinking in surprise.

"I know we talked about it, but I didn't think it would be so soon," I whisper, but before he can answer, Peter comes back. Wearing a furry panda head, he throws himself into the sex pit, which almost makes me gag. Who knows what's on all those cushions? He unzips his pants and pulls out his cock, fisting it in his hand before pumping it up and down a couple of times. He waves the gun that is still in his other hand.

"Get on with it. I put a bullet in Julia before I got a chance to use this stuff. If I wasn't worried about you getting knocked up, I would be taking this out on you, Harlow. Maybe I still will. If I fuck you in the ass, we won't risk you getting pregnant from me instead of him." His voice is muffled by the panda head, but I don't doubt he's serious. "Suck his dick so I can watch," he orders, and I shudder.

When Jaxon gives me a small nod that I hope Peter misses, I crawl back down his body. I lean over Jaxon's cock and run my tongue around the rim. He tastes salty, and I lick my lips before running it along his shaft. I think the drugs are making him more compliant because a loud groan leaves his lips even though I know he doesn't want to encourage Peter any more than we have to.

"Oh yeah, I want to see you choke on that dick, Harlow," Peter instructs, and I take it into my mouth. Sliding up and down, I suck on him a little before pulling away.

The sound of movement has me turning to look at Peter. He's removed his hand from his dick and is sitting up, his gun aimed at me. "Either do it properly or I will get in there and make you."

Goosebumps rise across my skin in fear, so I do as he's asked. Blocking him out, I resign myself to having to give the performance of my life. Taking

Jaxon's dick deep into my mouth, I gag, and my eyes water when it hits the back of my throat, but both Jaxon and Peter groan in unison.

"Fuck no." I sit up and put my hand on my hips, glaring at Peter. "I just can't do this with you watching and making noises. I'm sorry. It distracts me."

He scrambles out of the pit, his dick sticking out of his pants, and hurries over to the cocaine that's still sitting on the paddling bench. He sticks the gun into the hole and brings out the end of the barrel covered in coke. Then he heads over to the cage door, unlocks it with his free hand, and steps in. He shoves the gun in my face, and I freeze. My heart races. This is it. I'm dead. Fuck.

"Let me help lower your inhibitions a little because you *will* be fucking him right now, and I *will* be fucking watching. Snort," he demands. My eyes don't leave his as I lean forward and put my nose over the barrel. Blocking one nostril, I inhale the white powder and wait for my body to react to the drugs. I've never done anything harder than weed before, and I'm silently freaking out about what is to come.

Peter pulls the gun away from my head, but my heart doesn't stop racing. He backs out of the cage and slams it shut again.

"Sit on his face, Harlow," he commands. My body is starting to feel a little light. While my mind sharpens, the feel of Jaxon's skin on mine intensifies.

I slide my way up his body until my thighs are straddling his head, lowering my pussy to his mouth. The first swipe of his tongue through my folds has me throwing my head back in pleasure, my loud groan echoing through the room. I stop holding my weight and relax into what Jaxon is doing, his tongue licking and sucking as his nose nudges against my clit. He's moaning with delight as my hands shoot out to grip the metal bars of the birdcage in front of me. The sensory overload has me riding Jaxon's face like a cowgirl at a rodeo, the smooth slide of the metal bars under my hands just adding to the stimulation. It's like my mind has compartmentalized everything, so the fact that Peter is watching doesn't even register anymore.

My entire focus is on Jaxon and what he's doing to me. I can feel my orgasm building, that teasing feeling rushing at me like a freight train. My hands leave the bars to trail over my skin and up my stomach to my breasts, a tingle following in their wake. Cupping them, I pinch both nipples as my orgasm detonates.

"Fuck!" My hands leave my body, digging into my hair as I undulate over Jaxon's mouth, slurping sounds coming from him as he drinks down everything I give.

I'm ready for his dick now, and the need to have something inside my clenching cunt has me scrambling off him. When I look down, he's grinning up at me, his face glistening with the evidence of a job well done. Leaning down, I kiss him, and the sweet flavor of my release bursts to life on my tongue as it tangles with his. My teeth nip at his lip hard before I pull away and line myself up with his thick dick. Notching it at my entrance, I slam myself down on it as he thrusts up. His guttural groan is like a symphony for my ears as I throw my head back, screaming at the intrusion. My cunt is tight from my orgasm, so there's a swift bite of pain before it smooths out into a deeper pleasure.

Our eyes meet, and we start to move, my hands against his hard abs, rolling my hips as he thrusts up with his. There's a laser-focused intensity and what feels like a soul-deep connection—like he and I are one with each other. We don't talk. It's just a cacophony of grunts, groans, and moans as we drive ourselves higher and higher with each roll of my hips. Both of us are panting hard now, and I'm almost transfixed by the drop of sweat that rolls down Jaxon's temple. Leaning down, I catch the drop with my tongue, the salty flavor tingling in my mouth. I'm low enough that he does the same, his tongue licking between my breasts. Sitting back up, my orgasm is just out of reach. Frustrated, I lean my hands against Jaxon's chest, rolling my body harder, so his frantic thrust can hit my clit.

"Fuck, yeah, that's it, Harlow. I can feel your cunt. It's so tight. Get there, Harlow," he grits out, and I can see the muscles in his neck tightening. Just knowing that he's struggling to hold on to his orgasm is enough to tip me over the edge. My breathing starts speeding up, then I'm screaming as my orgasm ignites my senses. It's all I can do to hold on as he takes over. After a couple more violent thrusts, he's shouting too. I can feel his hot dick pulsing as his cum pours into me. Another groan leaves my mouth at that thought, and my pussy pulses, milking his cock dry. Leaning down, I kiss him like my life depends on it. Slow and sensual, I pour all my love into it, and I can feel him doing the same.

Slowly, my orgasm ebbs, as does his even though he's still rock hard inside of me.

Our bodies are slippery with sweat as I pull away from him, small residual shockwaves running down my limbs. My mind is racing a million miles an hour, and everything feels so much more.

"Oh my god, that was so good." I stretch my arms into the air, languishing in how I feel with his dick still buried inside me.

"You're not wrong. I wish I had time to take that ass for a spin." Peter's voice is low and rough, a thunderclap in the room.

I startle, having forgotten all about him because I was so hyper focused on Jaxon and what we were doing. Scrambling off Jaxon, I feel his cum run down the inside of my thigh. Peter's standing at the edge of the cage, one hand wrapped around the bar and the other around his cock. His eyes are locked on my pussy as his hand furiously pumps. His knees buckle slightly before ropes of cum squirt between the bars, landing on the floor at the end of my bed.

"Look at that," he chuckles as his hand slows. "Got it all on your panties, Harlow. Now you'll feel both of us when you put them back on." He tucks himself back into his jeans as I just blink, having no words for this disgusting man. "Okay, no time to put your legs in the air. You'll just have to fuck him again once we're done here. Leave him there while we go get my book," he orders, unlocking the cage and opening the door as I slide off the bed. Disappointment races through me at having to leave Jaxon behind.

"Hurry up, Harlow," Peter growls, stalking over to the door for the panic room and down the stairs. It's open, so he doesn't need me to program in the code.

Holy fuck. Did he just leave us alone? Ignoring the fact that I'm still naked, I quietly unbuckle the restraints around Jaxon's wrists and ankles, my heart racing and my stomach in my throat as I fumble in my haste. Jaxon is quiet, his eyes locked on the doorway, looking out for Peter.

"Harlow, if I have to come back up there, I'm putting a bullet between Jaxon's eyes, You can forget the baby-making scheme," Peter calls, and it echoes up the circular staircase clearly enough for me to hear the true threat in his voice.

Fuck, do I risk him coming back? I glance around for a weapon, but there's nothing really I can use.

"Go, don't risk it. We'll figure something else out," Jaxon whispers, and I stop what I'm doing, a defeated sigh slipping from my lips. Bending down, I grab the rest of my clothes off the floor, leaving my panties exactly where they are. There is no fucking way I'll put those back on now. Looking around for something to wipe myself with, there's nothing but the bedsheets, and I refuse to use those. I might have been able to ignore them while riding Jaxon's dick, but there's no way I'm going to use them to clean myself up.

Grabbing Jaxon's briefs, I swiftly make do. "Sorry, but leggings and dripping cum will make a bad situation *so* much worse," I tell him ruefully, and he chuckles.

"Anything for you, babe. I love you." His pupils aren't so dilated now, and he seems to have come down a little like I have, so there's an easy sincerity in those words that rings true.

'I love you too. I'll work something out," I promise as I hurry to pull my clothes on. When done, I give him a quick kiss. "Don't go anywhere," I joke, and his small smile is enough to get my feet moving. I will do anything to keep this man safe.

I hurry down the circular steps to the panic room, following the sound of Peter muttering to himself. When I get into the room, my movement slows as I pass the bed. The doors to the gorgeous thing are wide open, and the base is bare, the mattress having been removed. My heart warms at the realization that the boys have been here, and it reinforces that I can't let Peter win. I know the minute he hasn't got any use for me, I'll be dead. I'm a pawn, a puppet for him to twist my strings, and when he's got what he needs, he'll cut them permanently, which means Jaxon and I will be dead.

But in a startling moment of clarity, I realize I *have* come up with a solution. It's pretty easy, really. It's the same reason he needed one of the twins in the first place. Blood.

Chapter Seventeen

Harlow

"Hurry up, bitch. We need to leave." He sounds impatient, but there's a hint of anxiety there too, and who knows what kind of state his mind is in after all the coke he snorted. Jaxon and I only had a small amount compared to that. He's going to be wired for hours, and the last thing I need is for him to get trigger happy.

When I enter the closet, I'm surprised to find it empty except for some jewelry and various knick-knacks on top of one of the set of drawers. Peter is holding a gold watch in his hand, his eyes wide with awe.

"Look at this." He waves the gun around, making my heart skip a beat. "It's a Patek Phillipe.

Got to be worth six hundred K. I'm just going to take this. I'm pretty sure my uncle would have left it to me in his will."

This time, my heart just about seizes in my chest. Fuck! *The will.* That's one of the other documents in this safe, and we have no idea what it says. It might very well declare that in the event that he and Dragos passed on, Peter would be the sole beneficiary to the Bucătaru fortune. I need to make sure he doesn't see it.

Not wanting to draw this out any longer, I key in the code for the safe. The little beeps are loud in my ear but not as loud as Peter's fetid breath which washes across my shoulder as he tries to get a look at what I'm doing.

The safe clicks open, swinging the door wide. "Is that it?" he asks as he shoves me out of the way.

Fuck, fuck, fuck. He's pulling everything out before I can even attempt to. He shoves the gun that was in there into the waistband of his pants.

"Tut, tut, tut, Harlow, that was *very* naughty. You didn't say anything about the gun. Did you think you could get a shot off before me?" He no doubt knows that if I could get my hand on it, I would have shot him.

A phone beeps in his pocket, and when he pulls it out, his face pales.

"Fuck, that was Raquel. Someone has arrived at the work site."

He calls her as he gestures for me to grab everything else and get moving. "Get rid of them, Raquel, or you *and* them will get a bullet when I get down there." He hangs up without letting her speak a word, then shoves me. "Let's go."

I do as he says, and we hurry up the circular stone steps until we get back to the sex room. When he aims the gun at Jaxon, my whole world stops.

"Nooo!" I scream, knocking his arm off track. The bullet smacks into the wall on the other side of the room. Peter's backhand knocks me to my feet and rattles my brain before one hand wraps around my throat as the other rests the gun against my head.

"What the fuck did you do that for?"

I try to speak, but he's got his hand too tight. So instead, I'm gasping for air and scratching at his hand while trying to keep an eye on the gun at my head. He finally lets go a little, and I suck in a deep breath before panting.

"Blood! We might need his blood to get into any of the safes on the other properties." He lets go of my throat and steps back, a thoughtful look on his face. "It would be safe to guess that they have biometric scanners too." I meet his eyes and hope that he can't see how terrified I am. I'm going to have to play the will card now, too. I really don't want him to see it, but considering how obsessed the count was with his bloodline, I'm taking a flying leap of faith. I pick up the bundle of papers I had dropped while he was strangling me and wave them at him. "In my hand is the last will and testament of Count Bucătaru." He eyes the paperwork with greedy glee. "If it says what I think it does, we'll need to provide a blood-related heir to inherit it, so that leaves my womb and Jaxon's swimmers. Jacinta won't be as easily managed as her brother."

He stares at me for a moment before nodding. "Fine, release him. Then we're going back down and out the front door and across to where we left the car. I'll shoot anyone I see, so the two of you better not make a sound unless you want to be responsible for more deaths."

He's lost all the devil-may-care attitude he'd assumed since he'd snorted his coke, and now he's back in killer mode—which is very dangerous for the rest of us.

Without waiting, I scramble off the floor, passing him the papers. I don't actually care anymore. I just want to do everything I can to get me and Jaxon out of here alive. I would burn this house down if it meant that the two of us were safe.

Once he's free, Jaxon gets dressed, minus his underwear which are on my ass. As we exit the cage, Peter holds out two pairs of handcuffs. "Cuff each other," he instructs, and we do as he demands with no argument. Jaxon seems to be in survival mode too.

Before long, we've gotten out of the elevator and are back on the landing. I try to close up the secret doorway, but he just shouts at me to "Fucking leave it."

So we hurry down the two flights of stairs, the feeling of that gun pointed at our backs sending tingles down my spine. I hate not being able to see him; it makes me feel paranoid and jumpy.

We hurry across the entry hall, and when we get to the front door, I throw the lock and push the door open. The same hallway clock tells me we've been upstairs for less than an hour, and it's only 7:15 in the morning. But as we hurry over the draw-bridge and to the old access track, I can see a car driving away from the zoo. I breathe a short sigh of relief. I don't know what Raquel said to get them to leave, but I'm thankful now.

Jaxon and I burst out onto the track, stumbling over the uneven ground since the handcuffs are slowing our pace and throwing off our balance. I can see the car from here. I just hope we make it before anyone else arrives for work.

When we get there, I'm panting, sweat prickling on my brow, and neither Jaxon nor Peter are in much better shape than I am. Raquel is leaning against the car, looking a bit better than the last time we saw her. She must have found something to clean up with in the car.

"Who was it?" Peter asks.

"Some guy named Parker, said he worked for McCallister Construction."

And I thought my heart couldn't beat any faster, what with the jogging and my own panic, but hearing Parker's name just kicks it up into a level I never knew it could beat. Fuck, I hope I'm not having a heart attack. I exchange a look with Jaxon, praying that Parker is now on his way back across the road to talk to Dad about the jobs.

"I told him that there was a mix-up with permits, so he wasn't allowed to start today. I'm not sure he bought it, but he said he was going to check with the boss and would be back."

"Shit, okay." Peter pops the trunk. "Get in." He gestures to me and Jaxon, and we move to do as he says. At least we're kind of safe in the trunk.

"Where's Mom? Is she coming?" Raquel is looking down the track, and before either of us can answer, he swings his gun in her direction and fires. The look on her face says she never saw it coming. He shoves at us, and within minutes, we're stuffed in the trunk and heading back down the track, being jolted and bustled by the uneven surface.

"Do you think someone heard that gun shot?" I ask Jaxon once I finally calm my racing heart and heaving breath. I feel him shake his head. My back is to his front, and he's curled his face into my neck, seeking and giving the comfort that we both so desperately need.

"Probably not, " he mumbles, sounding as wrecked as I feel. Now that the adrenaline is leaving my body and the cocaine is wearing off, I feel like I've been hit by a steam roller. Everything aches, and I'm so fucking tired. "Harlow, I'm sorry I've been so fucking useless." Jaxon sounds so distressed; I nuzzle into him the best I can.

"Oh, honey, don't be. We need to do what we can to survive, and if that means playing possum and doing everything he instructs, we'll do that until we find a weak spot. Then we bomb the shit out of his plan and come out on top victorious."

"But I should be the one protecting you, not the other way around! Now I'm so freaking tired I can barely keep my eyes open. How is that any help?"

"Sleep, babe, we can't do anything back here, and who knows what Peter is going to do with us next. Let's get a little rest while we can." My stomach rumbles, and my mouth is dry. I desperately need a drink, but neither of us are going to get what we need for now, so sleep will only benefit us.

A small snore tells me Jaxon really wasn't kidding. I settle my body back against him, his warm and comforting and solid weight against mine. I allow myself a moment to soak in that feeling, thankful that both of us are still alive, and, despite having to perform sexually for a violent coke addict, no less worse for wear. I need a moment to regroup, then I'll come back swinging. Just as my eyes start to close, I hear a siren, but it fades into the distance. It must have been for something else. With that little bit of hope fading, I allow my eyes to close, and darkness sucks me in.

The sound of a slamming door jolts me from the deep sleep that I assume was helped along by the come down from the coke. I have no clue how long we've been asleep, but I don't feel like it's been long enough. I'm foggy and unfocused, and it's only the feel of Jaxon's body against my back that gives me any reassurance. There's a click, then the trunk opens ever so slightly before it widens, and I have to squint my eyes against the sudden onslaught of light. Peter's shadow is looming over us.

"Let's go." He hauls me out of the trunk, and as I steady myself, he does the same to Jaxon. When I finally get my bearings, I have a look around, and my heart sinks. Of course we aren't lucky enough to return to the previous house. No, Jacinta must have sounded the alarm by now. He must have had a back-up plan, but where the fuck are we? In front of us is a small cabin nestled amongst some big trees. I'm not familiar with California's vegetation, so I have no clue where we could be, and I don't want to ask Jaxon. I don't want to do anything that will set Peter off.

Jaxon grunts as Peter none-too-carefully pulls

him out of the trunk, and when he's on his feet, the door to the cabin opens. A woman steps out, and although she's familiar, I can't pinpoint where I've seen her before.

"Fuck me," Jaxon hisses as Peter moves up the steps of the cabin to gather her in his arms, kissing her full on the mouth.

What the fuck? I thought he was with Julia. Who is this woman? I raise my eyebrow, looking at Jaxon and the major glare he's sporting.

"That's Patricia, one of the attorneys that was part of the trust."

"Did you get it?" she asks breathlessly when they pull apart, and he has a smug grin on his face.

"I sure did." He runs back to the car and grabs the paperwork, waving it around as he returns to her side. She scowls as she snatches it out of his hand.

"So why are those two here?" She gestures to me and Jaxon, and Peter sighs.

"A contingency plan, of course. What if the rest of the properties have blood-linked security? We need the boy just in case, and as for the girl, well, in that little pile is the last will and testament for Count Bucătaru."

"The actual will? We didn't think there was one," she gasps.

"I was thinking about the chances of needing a blood heir to inherit. I can't do that, and that one won't share his inheritance with us," Peter parrots to her almost exactly what I said to him, making it sound like it was his idea. "I was thinking... Wouldn't it be better to have a baby that we could mold and shape like we want? Not to mention any child would need responsible guardians to manage the inheritance until they were of age, of course."

Patricia finally seems to grasp what he's saying. "Oh yeah, I get what you're saying, but why her?"

"She's convenient, and I made them fuck already, so hopefully—" He breaks off when she rolls his eyes.

"It doesn't happen that quickly, you dumb fuck. Seems a bit risky to me. Let's get rid of her. I'll fuck him and have the baby," she offers, leering at Jaxon like a dirty fucking cougar bitch. When I see Peter's mouth twist in anger, I angle my body in front of Jaxon in case he decides to pull his gun out again.

"No, we do it my way. Hurry up and get in here. Don't make me get my gun back out." Jaxon and I shuffle up the steps and into the small cabin. Peter shoves past us when we stop in the rustic living area. He pushes back a rug and lifts a panel in the middle of the floor. "In here," he orders, and I grimace when I see a set of steps leading to what I assume is the root cellar.

"I really need to pee," I tell him, but he shrugs.

"There's a toilet down there." I hold my hands out to him, and he fishes into his pocket for the key.

"What are you doing?" Patricia asks him a little shrilly.

"They can't get out from down there. They can have their hands back. Besides, Harlow is going to make sure she's knocked up otherwise I will have no use for her," he threatens, and I quickly agree.

"Of course, but I want my cut. You promised me." I flutter my eyelashes in the hope that I can provoke Patricia with a little jealousy, but when I glance in her direction, she's not even paying attention. She's flicking through the little black book, and when I see her mouth drop open, followed by a scowl, I know we're in trouble.

"It's missing the last few pages. They've been ripped out! The combinations for the rest of the safes are missing. Julia said they would be written in here. Where the fuck is Julia, anyway?"

"I got rid of the bitch and her useless daughters too. She fucked up. There was only one body recovered by the police. Dragos could still be alive."

"Fuck!" She hurls the little black book through the room. "This is all useless without those codes. Where the fuck could they be?"

Peter yanks my hands to him, unlocks my and Jaxon's cuffs, then pushes us down the steps. Neither Jaxon nor I have eaten or had anything to drink for thirty-six hours now. Add the cocaine to that, and the both of us are really in no condition to fight back. So we stumble down the stairs, helping each other, and I'm just glad neither of us trips or falls. A broken neck is not going to help anything.

The cellar lid drops down, plunging us into

darkness, but I had seen the cord to a light hanging as we came down. My hand brushes against it, so I give it a pull. The cellar lights up just as Peter and Patricia start a screaming match to rival anything my mother had with one of her johns.

Chapter Eighteen

Kai

My hands grip the steering wheel so tightly my knuckles are white as I push the car faster than the prescribed speed limit. Jake is in front with lights flashing and siren wailing as we fly toward our place. My eyes keep swinging back and forth to the clock, watching the minutes tick by agonizingly slowly. So much has happened that it feels like it should be the middle of the day, but the clock only reads 7:15 as we get closer to our destination. *Only another ten minutes.*

Thomas and Jake are going straight to our new place while the rest of us head to Dad's to update everyone.

Hopefully, Thomas has phoned ahead and warned the security team about a possible intruder. If we're right about their next step being a search for the book, they could be at our place or heading to Dad's. Depending on whether or not they trust each other, they might even split up and try to hit both places at once. There are just so many variables.

The silence in the car is excruciating. We're all lost in our own thoughts, and right now one of Oli's stupid comments would be most welcome. It would at least break the rigid atmosphere. I'm sure my brothers have the same toxic thoughts running through their minds that I have running through mine. *How could we let this happen? What could we have done to prevent it?* But really there are no answers that could make us happy.

We took every precaution, and it was our unfortunate luck that they found a way to wiggle in. I know Thomas will be flogging himself for not escorting them to the boat. But then we'd be missing another family member as well. And who knows if they would have left him alive. They probably wouldn't have taken any chances, so he would be a corpse on the side of the road. No, it's much better that he's here and able to be involved in the rescue.

Finally, I pull into our street and turn into Dad's driveway. The silence in the car is even more obvious now that the engine noise has gone. I can't stand it.

"Shit, will someone say something? Anything, I just can't stand the silence anymore." I turn in my seat so I can see Declan and the other two in the back.

"Sorry, I've been trying to work out everything in my head. There's so much to keep straight," Oli apologizes, and I feel some of the tension leave my body now that we're all talking again.

"Yeah, I was doing the same, but maybe we should have been talking it out amongst ourselves," Holden adds in, sighing loudly. "It's like something out of those soap operas that Mrs. H loves so much."

Declan is still quiet. I give him a nudge and he jumps, blinking as he looks at me in surprise.

"Hey, man, what's going through your mind? You were miles away."

"I was just thinking about Cecelia and what happened to her. I'm praying that the same thing won't happen to Harlow. Peter and Julia have a use for Jaxon, but Harlow is sort of dead weight. What if they've kept her to sell to their sex trafficking ring?"

My blood just about freezes in my veins. Fuck, I didn't think about that.

"We need to find them!" I slam my fist against the steering wheel before wrenching the car door open and heading inside, knowing that everyone is following me. The others all jump to their feet when we enter, and they throw questions at us all at once.

"Quiet!" I shout, unable to handle the noise.

"Let us tell you what's happened, then you can ask any questions."

So the four of us share what we learned while we were out, and Dad pales when we gets to the bit about Cecelia.

"That's horrible. The poor girl. Nobody deserves that. She was obviously a product of her upbringing," Nana voices. "If her family doesn't come forward to claim her body, we'll take care of her funeral expenses."

"Well, it's not like they *can* come forward, is it? Both her mother and sister are wanted for kidnapping," Oli points out.

"We can worry about that later," I tell them, trying to get them back on track.

"Dad, why don't you have a look for that book that Dragos gave you? I, for one, would like to know what's actually in it," Holden says to Dad.

"Yeah, okay, I'm pretty sure it's exactly where I left it in my bookshelf. Give me a moment." Dad heads back through the hallway to his office.

"I'll come with you... just in case," Chuck says, following after my father. He's right that it's probably not a good idea to split up.

Declan has his arm wrapped around Jazzy's shoulder as he whispers back and forth with her. Oliver and Holden are taking comfort from one another, and Melinda, Nana, Poppy, and Ben are all drinking coffee and talking quietly. Unlike them, I'm feeling twitchy and restless, and I can't fucking stand here. I need to do something. I'm just about to leave, wanting to see if Thomas and Jake have found anything, when Dad returns, a little black book in his hand.

"This is it." He flicks through it, and a couple of pieces of paper fall out with ripped edges.

I bend down and pick them up. Scanning them, it looks like letters and numbers. "What are these?"

- FR — 71419703, 01062021 , 70300205
- CO — 61590321, 55432190, 7 7654309
- RO — 88895437, 44456321, 00512389
- IT — 77704361, 67812345, 22212129
- CH — AB5678TS, JJJ90765, GHD6654
- US — 5318008
- KY — 19752601, 28195301,
- RU — 77553311, 6931512,
- GR — 6000213 , 5778000

Poppy, Dad, and Chuck peer over my shoulders at the papers in my hands.

"These look like country codes." Poppy points to the letters on the left side. "But I have no clue about anything else."

"Well, if the letters are country codes, then it's safe to guess the US is the States, especially since that's the code for all the safes in the house. We can probably assume the rest are codes to safes or safety deposit boxes or account numbers in all the other places the twins have inherited." Whereas the code made my brothers and I smile before, right now, it does nothing for me. I can't laugh at something juvenile like that while our woman is gone.

"Do you think these pages were ripped out of his father's book?" Chuck says to Dad before he sits back down with Melinda again.

Dad's phone rings. He hands me the rest of the book, and he answers it. "Hi, Miles, what can I do for you?" He frowns as he listens to him. "He *what?*" He starts toward the front of the house, and Chuck, my brothers, and Jacinta follow, hearing the urgency in his voice. "I'll call you back in a moment."

Dad goes into his office and enters the code to one of the gun safes. He starts pulling out weapons and passing them to each of us.

"That was Miles McCallister. He said Parker went over to the site earlier to get started, but some brunette woman turned him away with a bullshit excuse. She told him she was Harlow's PA. He thought it sounded a little weird, and so did his brothers when he asked them about it after he got back to the B&B."

"Raquel!" Jacinta gasps. "That means they're over there now."

"Yup, Thomas and Jake may need back-up, so we're going to go. I don't want to take the security in case they somehow get around us and come here. Jake's team is fifteen minutes out. They got caught up in traffic, and we can't wait. You stay here with Nana, Poppy, Melinda, and Ben," he tells our sister. I can see her getting ready to argue, but then she thinks better of it and returns to the living area to tell the others what's going on.

My heart races at the thought that Harlow might still be there, that she *was* there as we drove past. Fuck, we should have gone with Thomas and Jake. We were thoughtless, and now we can only hope our brother and girlfriend don't pay the price for our carelessness.

When we get over there, we can see Jake's car parked on the drawbridge. The door is wide open, and there's no sign of Thomas or Jake.

"How are we going to do this?" Holden asks as we walk up the steps. "There are so many rooms in this house. They could be hiding anywhere!"

Declan's phone rings. "It's Thomas." When we see Declan's shoulders slump, we know the news isn't good.

"Okay, yeah, I'll get Oli to take us upstairs to the panic room and the safe. We'll see if they got what they were after. I'll let everyone know." Declan hangs up and sighs deeply as he shoves his phone back into his pocket and the gun into his waistband.

"What is it?" Chuck asks, unable to wait. Thank goodness for him.

"Thomas and Jake went into the zoo to go through the tunnel from the tiger enclosure. They found Raquel's body on the access track. There was a bullet through her forehead and tire tracks leading away from her. The blood around her is fairly fresh, so it looks like we might have only missed them by a few minutes."

"Fuck!" Holden shouts and grabs at his hair, and Oli wraps his arm around him as if that will somehow keep him from falling to pieces.

"Jake and Thomas are still going to go through the tunnels to make sure, but they want us to check the safe."

"Okay, well, shall we go check on the little black book?" Dad asks, and Oli shakes his head.

"Ah no, Dad. I think it would be best if you and Chuck stay down here."

"Why? I want to go too," Chuck argues, and Oli looks at me like he wants me to step in. Why would he not... Oh, the sex room!

"Yeah, why don't you two head down to the vault and check out everything down there? You can meet Thomas and Jake when they get there," I suggest, grasping at straws in the hope that they will take it.

"Good idea. Come on, Chuck, let me show you how crazy the count was." Thankfully, Dad is as clueless as ever even though Chuck's eyeing the four of us like we're hiding something. I mean, we are, but I don't think Harlow would appreciate her other dad seeing our sex room. Especially because we have every intention of keeping it.

Once Dad and Chuck disappear down the elevator, the four of us hurry up to the next level.

As the elevator moves upwards, I can only pray that they didn't have enough time to grab the book. Otherwise, we've hit another dead end.

Chapter Nineteen

Jaxon

The fight above us gives way to sex sounds that thankfully disappear as they take themselves into the back bedroom.

Harlow and I both use the bathroom and gulp down mouthfuls of water from the tap in the sink. In the corner of the room was a pile of dusty blankets, so we shake them out the best we can, coughing and spluttering from the amount of dust in the air, then make ourselves a bed out of them. We're making the most of being released, resting with our arms wrapped around each other. No one knows what will happen next.

I feel *so* fucking guilty that Harlow has had to do all the heavy lifting so far. I've been completely useless. Her quick thinking has kept us both alive, but our luck is going to run out eventually. Patricia was all too interested in this baby daddy plan, which might mean a lot for my survival odds, but surviving won't mean much to me if Harlow is gone. No matter the circumstances—handcuffed, drugged, or whatever—there would always be a part of me that felt like I should have, could have, found a way to save her.

"Do you think they locked the hatch?" I whisper in her ear, and she only shrugs, not answering. Frowning, I roll her over to face me, but that doesn't make me feel any more settled. There are tears rolling down her face, and that hits me straight in the heart. She's been so strong. What can I do to help pick her back up again?

"Oh no, babe, don't cry. What's wrong? I mean, apart from the obvious." I wipe the tears, but they keep coming, so I wrap my arms around her and bring her into me.

"How are we going to get out of this? I'm so tired, and I feel like everything is hopeless, not to mention the fact that I practically *raped* you before! I feel sick." All the words tumble out of Harlow's mouth, the syllables practically blending together. It's like she needs to get it off her chest, or she might not get the chance to free that weight from her shoulders.

"Don't think like that. You've been so freaking brave. I'm the one who feels like I've let you down.

You've kept us both alive, and you even got Jacinta out. No matter what happens to us, you gave me such a gift. It's hard enough knowing that your life is still at risk, but the thought of losing both of you…" I have to take a moment to breathe, unable to finish that sentence. Instead, I move on to the next part. "And I'm pretty sure I was just as involved in the sex as you were. You didn't hear me complaining at all." I stroke her back and try to reassure her as best as I can.

Unfortunately, my dick doesn't catch on to the seriousness of the situation because he's decided to join the party. I shuffle my hips away from Harlow a little bit. Her body feels good, and remembering what we did earlier doesn't help, but now is not the time or the place. Thankfully, she doesn't seem to notice.

"Let's get some sleep so we're more alert for whatever comes next. They need to get the codes, or they're screwed, and you and I have no clue where they are. The only probability is that maybe Dragos had them. He's the one that is missing from all of this. "

"I don't know. It's like my brain can't string two sentences together, let alone come up with a plan." She shudders in my arms, her distress coming out in the subtle shake of her body.

"Shhh, it's okay. It's my turn to do the heavy lifting. You sleep, and I'll come up with an idea. It's the least I can do." I keep stroking her hair until I feel her body relax. Within minutes, she's breathing heavily, fast asleep. The coke really messed us both up. I never want to feel like this again.

I desperately try to come up with a plan, but my eyes keep closing too. *Maybe I'll just have a quick nap and things might be clearer when I wake.* I allow my heavy eyes to close, and it's lights out.

The hatch banging open has me sitting bolt upright, out of a deep sleep. My mind takes a little bit to catch up to my body, and when it does, I see Peter coming down the steps with a tray of food.

"Here, eat this. I need you both to get your strength up. We've come up with a plan. I remember Julia saying your bitch mother did a smash-and-grab when you guys were younger, and it occurred to me that maybe she wasn't as stupid as we thought. Bitch probably planted the pages on Brad so she'd have something to hold over our heads. Then she had to figure out how to clean up her mess and get them back once she realized just how valuable they really were." Peter shakes his head. "Poor Carmen trusted Julia, so I guess your mother really did fuck you guys over. If she was a better judge of character, you wouldn't be here right now. Shit sucks, doesn't it?"

Holy shit, he's right.

For a second there, he seems almost human, and I'm so wrapped up in my own thoughts about what he's said that I almost miss the taunting undertone. Even after I notice it, I can't tear myself away from my spiral.

If Julia hadn't betrayed my mom and dad, Jacinta and I could be living our lives so very differently. There never would have been any need for Brad to adopt us. We wouldn't know the rest of our siblings, and Harlow wouldn't be in our lives. I'm not sure how I feel about all that. On one hand, I wish we had known our parents, but on the other, I wouldn't want it any other way than it is now.

Peter places the tray on a small table, drawing my eyes and my focus. "This is what's going to happen. Tomorrow, you're going to call your pilot and give him a flight plan to Russia. Hopefully, that will bring your family and the police away from your house when they go to the airport to intercept the plane. We'll grab the book, then make a run for it to Mexico. From there, we'll get a flight to the Cayman Islands, clear out your bank accounts, then onto Europe."

Peter paces back and forth across the small space while I calculate the possibility of me tackling him to the ground. He doesn't have his gun with him, but even though he doesn't look like he works out since he has that wiry frame of a junkie, I'm certainly not in the best shape right now. The odds are not as firmly in my favor as I'd like. I don't want to make anything worse for us, but I will hate myself forever if I don't even try.

I slowly get to my feet once his back is to me, but when Harlow moans in her sleep, Peter whirls back around. He looks between me and Harlow, reaches into the back of his pants, and pulls out his ever-present pistol. Fuck.

"I hope you weren't getting any crazy ideas," he says. The words are delivered with a clear sense of calm even though I can see the crazy lurking in his eyes.

I shake my head. "No, I was just going to grab the tray for us." His eyes swing to the tray as his lips turn up in a smug grin. "Good, good. You both need your strength. Anyway, where was I? Oh yes. Once we get to Europe, we'll hide out in a little non-extradition-treaty country. I've got a friend who will help us out. I believe your brother Thomas has had a run in with him. Urie Sokolov is my back-up buyer for the supply contacts. Fucking Sergio got arrested thanks to your bitch of a sister. One of his guys just called me, said he's being charged with murder. Seems he might have gotten a little too frisky with Cecelia, so at least I have one less loose end to tie up." Thinking about what could have happened to Cecelia, I feel ill. This man just gets more and more disgusting. The only thing good enough for him is a bullet between the eyes.

"Anyway, now that Sergio has been arrested, I'll

negotiate a deal with Urie and make sure it includes long-term accommodations for us. Once they lose interest in searching for you and Harlow, we'll clear out the rest of your holdings."

Peter is unusually chatty as he paces back and forth across the room like he can't stand still. If I had to guess, I'd say he's indulged in a little more cocaine since he's waving his arms around like he's having a manic episode. I keep my eye on the gun he's now got in one hand as he moves, hoping that his finger stays off the trigger. My gaze drops to where Harlow is still sleeping. I can't believe she hasn't woken. I'm starting to really worry about her.

"What's wrong with her?" He gestures to the pile of blankets.

"I don't know. She was tired when we got here, not to mention we haven't eaten in days."

"Well, wake her and eat this. I can't have dead weight dragging us down. If she can't get her shit together, we'll have to go with Patricia's plan instead. Though she's a bit old to have any more children. Maybe she just didn't want anymore after she had Luke. Can't say I blame her for that."

With that bombshell, he heads back up the stairs, leaving me to soak in what he just said. Patricia is Luke's mother, and Peter his father, yet neither seems to care that he's dead or that Peter was the one who killed him. Fuck, who needs enemies when you have a family like this?

"Harlow honey, wake up." I reach out and give

her a little shake. She groans and rolls onto her back, cracking her eyelids and squinting at me.

"I'm so tired," she grumbles.

"Peter brought us food. You should eat something. You'll feel better." I help her sit up before grabbing the tray and bringing it back to our makeshift bed. I pass her one of the steaming bowls of stew, absently noting that it actually smells pretty damn good. I don't know if that's just because I'm so hungry, but I really don't care. Spooning some up, I blow on it before shoveling some into my mouth. Flavor bursts across my tongue, and I groan out loud with pleasure.

Harlow had been watching me carefully, but now that she's seen my reaction, she doesn't hesitate to do the same. Her eyebrows jump in surprise as it hits her taste buds.

"Holy shit, it's really freaking good. I think it's homemade," she says around her mouthful of food, but I don't respond. I'm too busy using a piece of bread to scoop up some more.

While we eat, I fill her in on everything Peter had divulged to me. But as I do, it's like she deflates in front of me.

"We'll work this out. I'm sure there will be an opportunity for us when we get to Dad's place. Even if we get Thomas and the rest of them out of the house, there's the security to contend with too. We won't be helpless despite what Peter thinks."

I can see hope in her eyes when I say that, which makes me feel the tiniest bit lighter.

We sit in silence for a little while, finishing our food, but eventually the silence becomes awkward again. How has it come to this? No, I will *not* let this break us. I take her plate, and together with mine I put it back on the tray. Unfortunately, they only gave us spoons, which are all but useless as a weapon.

After I clear away the dishware I pull her into my arms and lay us back down. All I can do right now is fill the emptiness with things that will remind her of our life together and everything that's to come, so I just start to talk to her—about my new cruise line venture, all the things that will be happening to the zoo over the next couple of months, the renovations in the house, and about Jacinta and her potential relationship with Jace, Alex, and Shane. I do all the talking to start with, but eventually I get her to engage. By the time we get to my sister, she's lost her melancholy. Then she starts in on Hope and moves around to the subject of Max.

I don't know how much time has passed, but I'm happy to see my upbeat and positive girlfriend returned to me. Depressed and sad Harlow is just too hard to take. I never want to see her look like that again, and I certainly never want to be the one responsible for that either. It must be late afternoon by now. I have no idea how long we traveled while stuffed in the trunk of the car, and I have no idea how long we slept for before Peter brought us food. There's no sense of time here. I can't tell if it's still light outside or not.

I can hear Patricia and Peter murmuring, but I can't make out any words, and there's been no more shouting or sex noises since the first lot. I've explored the basement, and there's nothing down here except for the pile of blankets, the table, and the bathroom. There aren't even any chairs to pick up and use as a weapon like Harlow did the first time. I'm just sitting back down in our pile of blankets when the hatch door opens once more.

Patricia appears, holding a gun. "Let's go," she orders the two of us. I help Harlow up, keeping me between her and the gun as we make our way upstairs. I know my safety is guaranteed for now. They need my blood, and they are fully aware of that, but Harlow may have become expendable.

When we get upstairs to the little living area of the cabin, Peter's sitting at a table with papers in front of him. He looks up at us, and his maniacal grin brings goosebumps to my skin.

"It's go time. Jaxon, call your pilot and tell him to be ready for eight. Tell him to file a flight plan to St Petersburg."

Shit! I grab the phone that he hands me, dial Neighpalm Air headquarters, and order them to have the plane fueled up. I don't know if I want

Peter's crazy plan to work so that our family is safe and out of the way or for this all to blow up so that Peter and Patricia get caught. I just don't want anyone hurt in the crossfire, but I have no idea how to keep that from happening.

Chapter Twenty

Declan

"Fuck, they've taken everything." Oli sounds despondent as we stare into the empty safe, practically mocking us with its lack of anything helpful.

We're at another dead end. I can't help but lose the small bit of hope I had been hanging on to, and when I observe my brothers, their defeated stances tell me they feel the same way. But as the oldest, it's my responsibility to keep them hopeful, so I get my shit together, taking a breath and clapping my hands to get their attention.

"Okay, let's get going then. I'm sure that Thomas and Jake will have come up with a plan by now." I'm grasping at straws, but maybe, just maybe, they'll have something—no matter how small the chance. If they haven't discovered anything, then we have no clues to go on. Peter and Julia have disappeared into thin air with Jaxon and Harlow in tow. The only hunch we have to go on is knowing they need the codes from Dad's book. But how they're going to get them, I have no clue—unless they decide to ransom Harlow and Jaxon for them. That would be the best possible outcome. They get the codes, and we get our family members back. Let's hope they decide to do that. I guess it's just a waiting game now.

"Are you okay?" Kai nudges me as we go up the stone staircase. Oli and Holden are in front of us, quietly talking to one another.

"Yeah, just running over our options in my head. Best case scenario is he ransoms Jax and Harlow for the codes in the book."

"Do you think he'll do that?" Oli turns back to look at us, and his hopeful look is heartbreaking.

"If he's smart, he will," I tell my brother, clapping him on the shoulder and giving him a quick hug. I need to be the emotional support for my brothers now. I can fall apart later.

Holden pushes the button, and we step inside the elevator. "That room is tainted now. I'm not sure Harlow is ever going to look at it the same again. Maybe we need to reconsider what we do with it."

"Let's just get them back to us safely. We can make any other decision later," I suggest as we start downward. He's not wrong, but that's a future worry.

The four of us move as a team from one elevator to the other. Again, Oli puts in the code, and we move down into the subterranean levels of the mansion. Down in the vault, we find Thomas and Jake. They're looking down at something, which of course has the rest of us rushing forward.

"Well, shit, this feels a little like déjà vu except this one's a lot fresher than the last one." Oli sounds like he's ready to run screaming, but I see him gritting his teeth and standing his ground.

"Who is that?" Holden asks what we all want to know.

"It's probably not too wild a guess to assume this is Harlow's aunt Julia. It looks like Peter may be getting rid of all the dead weight. First Luke, Sergio took care of Cecelia for him, and now both Raquel and Julia," Thomas says matter of factly.

"I need to go upstairs so I can get enough reception to call in these bodies," Jake says, looking at his phone.

"There's nothing else for us down here. Let's go up, so you can make that call. You can bring your guys in through the tunnels again. Maybe you could ask for the same team that came and got the count. Let's limit the amount of people who know about the tunnels if possible," I suggest, and Jake's quick to agree.

When we get back upstairs, Holden and Oli

disappear into the kitchen to make coffee while Thomas shows Jake to the office for some privacy.

Kai and I both head back to the sitting room we were in the day of the tour. How long ago was that now? It feels like forever. My brother's sigh is loud as we both take a seat, and I grab the decanter that we'd left behind the last time. There's not a lot in the bottom, but there's enough for Kai and me to have a drink. God knows we need it.

"What now, Dec?" Kai asks quietly.

"I wish I knew, Kai. I wish I knew," I pass him his glass, and we silently sip while we wait for the others to catch up with us.

Thomas

Jake uses the office to make a call to the office and get the crime scene crew in. I've already collected samples from the sex room for them to examine, so they don't need to go upstairs to examine the room. I'd really rather no one else knows about that secret elevator. There's already way too many who know about the tunnels and how to access the vault. The sooner we can get a big cat into that cage, the better. Then that will block off any access people may have. I make a note to ask them to start work on those enclosures first.

Once he's finished with that, he makes another call, this time to the detective in charge of Luke's case back in Connecticut. He fills him in on what Jacinta told him so that they can close his case over there, but just as he's finishing up, the detective says something to him. Jake's eyes widen, and he turns to me.

"Thank you for letting me know. I think you may have given us our first solid lead. I'll let you know if it pans out." He hangs up, looking excited, which is a relieving breath of fresh air. I've been kicking myself about missing Harlow and Jax by only a few minutes. Raquel's body was still warm and pooling blood when we arrived. We must have passed them on the way, but without knowing what kind of car Peter drives or what he looks like, we're out of luck. With only Chuck's basic description of him to go on, he sounds like nothing more than an ordinary man.

"Detective Jones said they found Luke's birth certificate. They were able to confirm that Peitre Baciu is his father, but the mother's name is what was most interesting. Her name is Patricia Williams, and she works for the law firm that managed the count's estate."

"Holy shit! Have we got an address for her?"

"No, but I'll get the tech guys working on it. They'll tear apart her life until we get something solid."

"Hopefully, unlike the others, she's using her

real name. She'd have to if she's been practicing law. There will be a record of her somewhere, and maybe she has a house they're hiding in."

My heart sinks again. "Unless she uses a shell company to buy property."

"I have a gut feeling we're getting to the end of the tunnel, so to speak." I appreciate Jake's attempt at reassurance, but that's all I've got in me—appreciation. I honestly can't say that I believe him.

"I'm going to take my brothers back to our dad's place. Keep me updated on the Patricia thing. Let me know if you get any leads."

"Yeah, I will do that. I'll head over there once the crime scene crew finishes here. I'm pretty sure your father's house will be the next target if they need those codes. I'm going to get a few undercover agents on your security team, so we're ready if they make a play for them."

Blowing out a big breath, I nod. "Okay. I'll see you later then."

Once he has the keys and directions to lock up, I go off in search of my brothers. Later that afternoon, Chuck and Melinda return to their own home with our promise to let them know if we hear anything. Melinda had been pale and looking unwell the whole time they had been here, so Nana insisted she go home to rest.

They'd been trying to get hold of Maxine to tell her about Harlow, but she hasn't been answering her phone. That, of course, caused an expected amount of panic until I told them what she had asked me to do. I couldn't let them go on thinking she was missing too. They were understandably shocked by their daughter running off since as far as they knew they were supposed to be meeting her for lunch the next day, but we finally got a response from her that confirmed she was well and would face the music with them in a few days.

Once they left, we all kind of drifted apart. Everyone's feeling a little lost while waiting for Jake to finish up over at the other house. With two different crime scenes to process, it was late afternoon by the time he came over and finished integrating his agents into the security detail.

The house feels like it's covered in a cloud of fog. Everyone is subdued and miserable. Jacinta is barely consolable, swinging between tears and anger-filled rants about how she could have done more. When Holden spoke to Hope, she wanted to come out, but he insisted she stay at her apartment in the city. We need one less person for us to worry about, and it will be easy enough to keep her updated via phone. It's not like we're drowning in progress.

All of us are hanging out in the living area while Mrs. Heyton bustles about trying to feed us and keep us supplied with coffee. Ben has retired to Nana and Poppy's wing of the house to pack. I think he felt uncomfortable and in the way. Poor guy, I'm sure it's not the reunion they expected. I overheard them talking, telling him to return home. I know they plan to visit him once everything is settled, but they've all still got to be pretty disappointed.

Meanwhile, I have my laptop open in front of me. Jake and I are waiting for everything the tech team found on Patricia, including a couple of addresses for properties in her name. My email pings, telling me the information has arrived just as Dad's phone rings.

I don't pay any attention to what he says as I open up the file, but his shouting has me looking up before I've really gotten to check anything out.

He puts down the phone, his eyes alight with excitement. "That was Chris. He wanted to ask me about a flight plan that Jaxon just filed. He said it was for eight this evening, but he wasn't sure if he could find a pilot in time since he and James are off for the next week."

"They must be trying to leave the country." Declan stands up from the couch. "We can't let them do that."

I frown and exchange a look with Jake, noting he looks as perplexed as I feel.

"That doesn't seem right. Why would they leave the country without the codes to all the vaults?" I ask him.

"Maybe they plan on hiring a safe cracker? Or blowing them up. It works in our favor if they're trying to make a run for it. I could have them surrounded by international authorities within hours. Where did the flight plan say they were going?" Jake asks Dad.

"Russia." Jake and I exchange another look.

"That's weird. The twins don't have any holdings in Russia. Or none that were in the trust, at least."

"Yeah, but the will might actually say something different. Maybe it mentioned off-the-books places," Oli says.

"You and Harlow never read it?" I ask my brother, and he shakes his head.

"No, then we didn't have to lie about what it said."

"Yet you lied about its existence," Kai drawls dryly.

I ignore their bickering; there's nothing that can be done about it now. There's something tickling the edge of my mind, a thought that I just can't grasp. Something is telling me that this is all wrong.

"What if it's a ploy to get us out of the house?" Holden says from where he's sitting. He's got an arm wrapped around Jacinta, though it's not doing as much good as it normally would. "Maybe it's just some kind of distraction?"

They all start to chatter, but I ignore it and sit down, reading over the information on Patricia. It lists her as owning three properties—an apartment in the city, a house in Connecticut, and a cabin about an hour from here.

"Hey, hey!" Jake shouts, holding up his hand to quiet my family. "This is what's going to happen. They'll probably be watching the place to see that you leave, so I would suggest that Thomas and the rest of you guys be seen getting into your SUV and driving toward the airport. If it's a ploy to get you out of the house, we need to sell it."

"But what if they're actually going to be there?" Jacinta interrupts.

"I'll have agents there to make sure the flight can't leave," he assures her. "Then I and the rest of our agents here will wait for them to arrive. We'll have this wrapped up by nightfall."

"I think that we should check out Patricia's cabin. Maybe they're holding Jaxon and Harlow there," I suggest to Jake, pointing to the information on my laptop.

"That actually sounds like a good idea. Even if they aren't, we may find another lead. Though hopefully they'll tell us once we have them apprehended."

The tension in the room seems to lift a little now that we have plans, but I still can't help but feel we're missing something.

Chapter Twenty-One

Harlow

While Jaxon called Chris and told him to have the plane ready, I managed to catch a glimpse of the clock when we were upstairs. It's five in the evening.

Of course, we did manage to get some valuable information from Peter and Patricia's next argument: I was coming along as insurance for Jaxon's behavior and my hostage potential, they were still undecided about using me for this baby-making plan, the will named Dragos as the heir, and yes, there was that pesky bloodline stipulation keeping Peter away from all of his hopes and dreams. It also apparently named a couple more properties that the trust had known nothing about, one in Russia and an island off the coast of Greece.

They've circled back to arguing about the baby plan when the hatch slams down over us again.

I'm standing there, staring up at the now closed hatch, trying to listen in on their argument, when Jaxon's arms snake around my waist. My back is tugged against his front as he nuzzles past my hair into my neck.

"Have I told you lately how much I love you?" he whispers, and my hands come up to cover his as I lean my neck to the side.

"Yes, but it's always nice to hear it. I'll never get sick of it," I tell him before turning around and winding my arms around his neck. "And if we ever get out of here, I'm going to spend the rest of my life showing you how much. You and your brothers are going to be the most loved men in the world," I promise him.

His lips meet mine, and we kiss, blocking out everything else around us, just enjoying the moment for ourselves. A small moment of peace in a chaotic and stressful world.

"You know it's my birthday in a couple of weeks," he says, not pulling his lips away from mine.

"Really, so is mine. When's yours?" I ask. This time I pull away so I can look at him, his handsome face staring down at me with such love.

"October thirty-first. Jacinta and I are Halloween babies. Mom used to call us her little monsters when she was in a good mood." My mouth drops open in surprise, and I gape at him. "What?" he asks.

"So is mine! That's pretty cool."

He beams at me. "Holden and Hope usually throw a star-studded Halloween party at one of our clubs, but what about if you and I went out to dinner and then back to my place in the city for a little bit of our own costume party?" His voice drops in a way that's all seduction, and my body shivers for an entirely good reason.

"That sounds acceptable," I tell him calmly, not wanting to show him how thrilled I am about going on a date with him. This has all happened so fast, and apart from my zoo date with Thomas, none of us have really done this the traditional way. Inwardly, I'm screaming and jumping up and down like an excited teenage girl. But then a thump upstairs breaks into my reality, and all that excitement drains away. "Providing we all get out of here alive."

"I have no doubt that we will. Have faith in our brother and his friend. Jake and Thomas know what they're doing. They'll find us. And we're about to go to them. They're not stupid enough to fall for the plane thing even though Peter and Patricia are stupid enough to think they will." He keeps his forehead pressed against mine. "They're going to have to leave soon. I heard Peter say it's a an hour drive back to our place. If we get separated, be careful. Make sure you come back to me."

"I'm not sure how they think they're going to get past the security on the property. Surely they know they're there." I snuggle into his chest, leaning my head against him.

"I don't know either, unless they're going to shoot their way through. But that will probably attract more attention than they want."

"From who?" I scoff. "There's no one around for miles. Chuck and Melinda are Dad's closest neighbors, and they're still a long way away. And I really don't want them caught in the crossfire either."

"Hopefully, no one is home when they get there. If they're smart enough to realize the flight plan is bogus, they'll have a contingency in place—maybe agents planted around the property or something. Or maybe everyone will decide to go to the airport so that the house is empty and everyone is safe. I don't care if they get the codes. I care about my family." His voice starts to break on that last word, making his distress clear, and I feel the same way. I've never had too much family to care about in the past, but now that I've got them, I want to make sure that they're safe.

Upstairs, Peter and Patricia go quiet. They've obviously come to a decision because the hatch opens again. "Harlow, get your ass up here," Peter demands.

"No, take me!" Jaxon pushes me behind him, which doesn't make me feel any better. I don't want him sacrificing himself for me, no matter how noble he might think he's being. A dead white knight does nothing for me. I need him alive, damn it.

"Move, Jaxon, or I'll shoot you," Peter says to him.

"You need me." Jaxon snaps back. "You won't shoot me."

"Do I? Or should I just take your sexy sister while we're getting the codes? I'm sure it won't be too hard to have her around."

My stomach lurches, and I reach my hand out, pressing it against Jaxon's back. "Don't, babe. They need both of us. We don't want to drag Jacinta back into this. I'll go." Even though I know the rational part of him would agree, I physically have to move him out the way. Poor Jaxon, such a hard decision —me or his sister. It's better that I take that choice out of his hands.

But Jaxon won't listen. He pushes me to the side and lunges for Peter. I don't know what's louder, my scream or the sound of the gun going off in Peter's hand.

Jaxon reels backward, his mouth open in shock as he looks down at his chest. A dark stain spreads out before he goes down on one knee. I lunge for him, but Peter grabs my arm, holding me back. All I can do is watch, practically hypnotized by the sight of my lover on the ground, blood bubbling out with each cough and exhale.

"No!" I scream, thrashing against Peter, but he has too strong of a hold on me.

"I guess we're going to have to nab the sister too," he says before towing me up the stairs. I can't take my eyes off Jaxon until Peter kicks at the hatch. It slams down, cutting him off from my view. The last thing I see is Jaxon's body falling forward.

I start flailing my arms, kicking and screaming at this horrible man. How could we have missed the signs of what he truly was? He was around us for years, yet we never realized he was a psychopath. If only we'd seen the truth, none of this would have happened.

Pain rips across my skull as Patricia grabs my hair and yanks me off Peter. He cocks his fist back and slams it into my jaw. Pain explodes, then darkness takes over.

My head and jaw are throbbing when I wake, stuffed into the back of their fucking trunk *again*. Tears stream down my face as I remember my last view. Jaxon! One of the loves of my life, gone. How am I supposed to go on? He was killed trying to protect me. How is Jacinta ever going to look at me again when she finds out I killed her brother, her twin? How are *any* of them going to be able to look at me again? I wish he'd killed me, too.

Sobbing, my body shudders, unable to control myself. I don't care what happens now. This has gone on too far; the cost has been too high, My mother, Luke, Cecelia, Raquel, Julia, and now Jaxon. It's too much.

Gritting my teeth, I get a hold of myself, a wave of ice cold fury washing through my veins. I'll mourn later, but now, I plot. They haven't tied me up this time; I guess they figured it wasn't necessary since I was knocked out. I feel around in the truck for something I can use as a weapon, my heart racing when the car slows, but then it bumps up and down like the first time we went to our place. Why would we be going back there? Surely that place is crawling with agents now, and they know there's no other book there.

My heart sinks as the car stops because I haven't been able to feel anything I could use as a weapon. I was hoping for a tire iron or a crow bar, but I guess that was just wishful thinking. When the trunk finally opens, Patricia grins gleefully at me.

"Behave, Harlow, or I'll put a bullet in every family member I see. Just like lover boy." If there was anything she could say to keep me in line, this was it.

When she helps me out of the trunk, I look around, but I don't recognize where we are at all.

"Where are we?" I ask them as she pushes me along after Peter. He's leading us into a grove of pine trees, which totally isn't the perfect place to dump a body or anything like that.

"You obviously haven't explored every part of this property yet," Peter calls back as the trees surround us. They're so close together that not much light gets through. The bright moon-lit night is filtered through dense branches, so it's almost as if there's no moon. Peter curses as he trips over something on the ground, then he rights himself, his phone in his free hand. The flashlight app shines, lighting up a little shack in front of us. It looks like an old wood shed or something. Peter tries to pull the door open, but tree debris has built up around the door, making it hard. He curses and uses his foot to pull everything away, finally yanking the door open. Inside the shack is a concrete box with familiar-looking elevator doors. He pushes a button, and it lights up. I can hear the whirring of machinery, and before long the doors open to us.

Patricia shoves me in after Peter before squeezing herself in. There's not a lot of room, so it's a snug fit, but the doors close behind her, then we move downward.

"This is one of the escape tunnels. It leads back to the house, but there's another that branches off and leads directly under your dad's place, coming up on the far side of it. The back of your dad's property has a matching shed just like this one. We'll come up there and have the element of surprise because no one will be expecting us. Idiots think it belongs to the gas company. I guess money doesn't buy intelligence."

The elevator doors open, bringing us into the tunnel system. There are no automatic lights in this one, so Peter continues to use his flashlight app to light our way. Before we go any further, though, Patricia yanks me to a stop. She's got a bag over her arm, and she pulls a roll of tape out of it.

"Sorry, Harlow, can't have you making any noise to give us away." She smirks as she pulls off a piece of tape, practically slapping it across my mouth, then she ties my hands together with cable ties. "Right, let's get moving."

I don't know how long we walk. It feels like hours, but it can't have been all that long. When we exit the shack, the moon is high in the sky. A sound has me looking up to the sight of the family helicopter winging away from Dad's home.

"Yes!" Peter whisper-yells. "They fell for it. Come on, let's hurry. I want to be in and out."

"We don't even know where the book is," Patricia hisses as we follow after him. The ground is uneven, and it's hard to go fast because I keep stumbling.

"Carmen told Julia the only room they weren't able to ransack was Brad's office. It was locked the day they broke in, and they didn't have time to break the door down. That's where we'll start."

"Why did Carmen tell Julia all those things?"

Patricia asks exactly what I had been thinking. How stupid was the twins' mother?

"Carmen thought they had a solid partnership even though she had betrayed Julia by giving the twins to Brad. She never outright said she was looking for a book, and she probably thought Julia was too stupid to realize the break-in was about more than just making an easy buck. Now that we know the book we have is incomplete, this is the only answer. Lucky for us, with both Julia and Carmen out of the way, it's more profit in our pockets." Peter's tone is gleeful, the sick bastard.

Again, Peter is happy to share everything in front of me. I just know I'm not going to get through this alive, whether he shoots me or because they sell me off into their trafficking ring when I don't end up pregnant.

I look around us, and I finally recognize the cross-country course that we had ridden what feels like years ago now, though in reality it was only a few weeks. A few weeks since Holden had been shot. God, I was responsible for that, too, even though it was Luke who pulled the trigger. I'm just toxic for this family. If we all somehow get out of this alive, I'll move far away, run a little practice in some podunk town, and be an old cat lady. I'm sure they'll be able to find homes for the cubs and Nyx. I don't think I could stand to live in the house Jax gave me without him.

The tape stops another sob from leaving my

mouth, but the tears continue to stream down my cheeks as I blindly follow Patricia and Peter. They must have made this trek before because they seem to know where they're going. Finally, we make it to the stables, and I peek up at where I know there's a camera. The little red light is blinking, and I can only pray that there's someone monitoring the feed full time at the moment.

As Peter peers around the corner of the building, Patricia yanks me close. "Remember, one wrong move and you will be responsible for the deaths of anyone we come across."

"Let's go," Peter whispers, gesturing for us to move. Patricia keeps her gun at my back. As we cross the open section of grass that's used as the helipad, I frown. Where's all the security? There should be at least someone positioned on the back patio, if not a couple more, but there's no one.

There are lights on in the living room, but I can't see anyone in the house. We creep past the pool and across the back patio until we get to the glass doors. They're closed, but they easily open when Peter tries the handle. The *click* is deafening to me, like a gunshot, but the space around us remains disappointingly empty. Goddamn it, why don't we have a dog? A big vicious attack dog. Patricia pushes me through the doors, and Peter gestures for me to go ahead.

"You first. Take me to your dad's office." There's nothing to do but bring him where he wants me to go. I look at one of the cabinets that I know hides a gun, but I can't take the risk that there might be people in the other wings of the house. If I tried for it, Patricia wouldn't hesitate to shoot anyone who interfered.

So I lead them down the hallway, praying no one is in there and that they may be distracted enough that I can get my hands on the gun in his bottom desk drawer. How I'll manage that with my hands tied is a problem for future Harlow.

Breathing deeply through my nose, I push the door open and step in.

Chapter Twenty-Two

Oliver

What would have taken us an hour by car takes us a little over twenty minutes in the helicopter, with Kai pushing it as fast as it could go. We come down next to the little shack, and we all jump out, guns at the ready. All of us are wearing vests provided by Jake and Thomas.

No lights can be seen, and no one comes running out of the shack. I look around and can't see a vehicle either.

"Maybe no one is here," I whisper.

"Declan, you and Kai go around the back to see if there's a back exit or windows anyone can climb out of. Holden and Oli, you're with me. Keep your eyes sharp. Watch out for Harlow and Jax, but assume anyone coming at you is unfriendly,"

Thomas orders, and I swallow, trying to clear a lump in my throat.

My nerves are shot and my heart racing, but there was no way I was going to stay behind. All of us Summers kids have practical experience with guns, but it's been a while since I've been to the range, and I can't say that I'm not nervous about pointing it at a live target. But if Jaxon and Harlow are here, I want to help rescue them.

Declan and Kai disappear around the back as instructed, and Thomas puts his boot into the front door. The flimsy fixture flies open, practically falling off its hinges. He swings his gun around in an arc, Holden going in behind him to cover his back. I reach around the door frame and blindly feel for a light switch. When I feel it, I call out to warn them that it's going to get a lot brighter in here.

I flick the switch, and the room lights up, showing us nothing. My heart sinks. A noise in the back has us all turning toward a small hallway, but it's just Kai and Declan.

"The rooms are empty," Kai says and drops his gun to his side.

"Fuck!" Thomas shouts and kicks at a coffee table in the middle of the floor. It tips over and drags the rug back with it. When I look closer, there seems to be a handle in the floor.

"Wait! Look at that," I point out, going over to it.

I check that my brothers are covering me before

I bend down to inspect it. They've all got their guns facing the hidden hatch. Lifting it, I pull it back. I can't see what they're looking at, but Holden swears and shoves his gun in his pants, running down into the cellar. Thomas isn't far behind, but Kai goes deathly pale and runs outside.

"What?" I let the lid drop down to the ground and go around to look. Declan has pulled his phone out and is calling someone. When I see what they're looking at, my knees nearly give way.

Jaxon is face down in a pool of blood. My heart races, and there's a sense of vertigo that almost overtakes me, my stomach pulsing with nausea.

"No." The word barely leaves my mouth as Holden reaches down and checks for a pulse. That feeling of déjà vu slams into me, recognizing we did the same thing to him not long ago.

I hold my breath, not hopeful with the amount of blood surrounding him.

They roll him over, and Thomas puts his hand over the wound, trying to stem some of the blood.

"I've got a pulse!" Holden shouts. The relief is brief as I hear the helicopter wind up again. "We need to get him to the closest hospital."

"They're sending the coordinates to Kai. It's ten minutes by helicopter. Let's go. They'll have a team waiting to receive him." Declan runs down the steps, and between him, Thomas, and Holden, they lift our brother and carefully carry him out to the chopper.

I look around the room, but there's no sign of Harlow, so I say a little prayer that she's safe. We'll get Jaxon fixed up, then we can continue our search for her. She would kill us if we let him die.

I chuckle at my thoughts, realizing I'm probably a little hysterical. But really, who wouldn't be at this point? How much stress and worry can we go through in the course of a day before we all start to crack?

"Oli, let's go!" one of my brothers yells, and I run after them. We lay Jaxon across the floor of the back, and within seconds of slamming the door closed, we're lifting off. Kai doesn't even wait for me to get my ass in a seat.

Declan searches one of the storage sections under the seat and grabs a first-aid kit. He pulls out a wad of bandages and hands them to Holden. When Thomas moves his hands away for a moment, he shoves them over the wound. The pristine white bandages slowly turn deep red as Thomas holds them down, maintaining pressure.

"It's not pumping out blood too fast, so that's a good thing, but from the sound of his breathing and the blood around his mouth, I'm assuming the bullet punctured his lung. We need to get him to a hospital. I'm not sure how much longer he's got." Declan grabs one of those masks that has a breathing bag at the end, and even though his face looks poised and calm, his hands have a shake to them that says otherwise. Thomas, on the other hand, sounds panicked, and it does nothing good inside me to know that two of my big brothers are freaking out. Dec slips the mask over Jaxon's mouth and starts squeezing the bag. I'm honestly not sure what it's supposed to do, but our wounded brother's breathing is ragged and slow, so I'll sit back and let the others do anything that they think will help.

"Oli, get my phone and text Jake. Tell him what's happened. They've got to be headed for Dad's, or maybe the airport thing was real."

I do as he says, asking a question of my own in the meantime. "But why would they go without Jaxon? They need his blood." The words are barely out of my mouth before an answer comes to me. He's not the only one with the right bloodline. I'm pretty sure it hits us at the same time if the looks on my brothers' faces are any indication.

"Fuck, they're going to try to take Jazzy too!" Declan yells as he continues to help Jaxon breathe. I follow up with another message to Jake before shoving his phone in my pocket. There's only so much we can do right now, no matter how terrible we feel, and Jaxon needs us focused on him if he's going to make it.

"How long, Kai?" Thomas shouts over the sound of the rotor. None of us have had a chance to put on a headset.

Kai doesn't hear him, so I grab one and shove it on my head. "Kai, Tom wants to know how long."

Kai looks down at his instruments. "Ten minutes," he tells me.

I hold up my hand and show them ten fingers.

"Fuck, I don't think we have ten minutes. Come here," Thomas orders as he reaches into the first-aid kit and pulls out a field transfusion kit. "Hold out your arm, Oli. You're the only one of us with O-neg blood. Jaxon needs some, or he's not going to make it to the hospital. He's losing more blood than he can afford."

Thomas wipes a bit of sanitized gauze over Jaxon's arm and slips the cannula into his vein before tying a tourniquet around my bicep and doing the same to me. There's a pinch as he slides the other end of the field kit into my vein. Once done, he releases the tourniquet, and my blood slowly works its way through the tube and into my wounded brother.

Holden monitors his pulse while Declan continues with the breathing bag as we all silently wait to reach the hospital and much needed help.

A medical team meets us in the parking lot with a gurney as Kai sets the chopper down. It's been cleared, and there are police cars keeping people away, which has to be thanks to Tom and Jake's connections. I climb out first as Holden and Thomas help the doctors get Jaxon onto the bed.

A doctor takes over for Dec, assuring he will take care of him, and my big brother sags to the ground, adrenaline draining away now that we've reached help.

"Okay, let's go. Can you keep up?" one of the doctors asks, and I nod.

"Once we get him into the OR, we'll replace you with a proper blood bag, but I don't want to disconnect you until we do."

"I'm okay. I'll be fine." I run along with everyone else as doors slam open, the group of us rushing through the corridors of the hospital. That distinctive smell of disinfectant and sadness hits me like a sledgehammer, and I almost stagger, but I manage to hold myself upright. I will *not* fail Jaxon now.

We make it into a surgery room, and they finally come to a halt. On three, they move him from the gurney to the table. I don't know if it's the adren-aline, the blood donation, or both, but I'm starting to feel a little dizzy. A hand on the arm without the needle has me looking at someone other than my brother. A nurse with kind eyes helps me into a wheelchair, and I think she says something to me, but I can't comprehend anything. There's only the rush of blood in my ears, then the slow beeping of the cardiac machine when they hook my brother up. Bags of blood and saline are hung, his arms both hooked up to the life-saving fluids he desper-ately needs.

The doctors are shouting orders, but they finally

remove my transfusion needle from him and wheel me away. I want to fight to stay, but I know that right now, I'm a hindrance. I need to let them do their job. I'm wheeled into my own room where I'm helped into a gown and put into a bed. It's not long before I have my own saline drip, a glass of juice, and orders to rest. My brothers descend on my foggy silence, looking absolutely wrecked. Thomas is still covered in Jax's blood, and the other three don't look any better.

"Jax?" I ask, trying to sit up, but Holden puts a gentle hand on my chest and pushes me back.

"We haven't heard anything. We thought we'd wait in here with you. They know where we are when they need to find us," Declan tells me.

"I'm probably going to get into trouble for leaving the helicopter in the parking lot," Kai says as he stares out the window.

"Is it blocking the ambulances?" Declan asks, rubbing a hand across his face, his exhaustion matching the rest of us.

When Kai shrugs, Dec replies, "Oh well. We'll donate some money to them. They'll get over it."

"Has anyone told Dad what happened?" I ask him, and they exchange a look.

"Jake messaged back—said they were radio silent and not to message Dad. I'm pretty sure he turned his phone off," Thomas growls, but I know he's not angry at me. This situation has all of us tied up in knots. Not knowing if Jax is going to survive or what's going on at home is awful.

All we can do is pray that the doctors here and Jake and his agents there will be able to save our family.

Chapter Twenty-Three

Harlow

Dad's office is dark, so I fumble with my tied hands to find the light switch on the wall near the door until the room lights up. No one is here, and my stomach drops. Where is everyone? Did they really fall for the plane thing? Jaxon was sure they wouldn't.

Patricia pushes me away, heading straight for the bookcase, and starts pulling out book after book. Peter heads for the desk and starts rummaging through the drawers. There goes my opportunity to look for a gun.

"Where is it? It's got to be here!" Patricia mutters as she continues to fling books onto the ground. I lean against the wall as Peter gives up on the desk, stomps over to me, and rips the tape off my mouth.

"Tell me where it is!" he shouts at me.

"How the fuck should I know? I didn't even know he had it." I try to sneer at him despite my lips and skin stinging where he'd ripped the tape away. He backhands me, and I smack my head against the wall. I slump against the wall with a groan as he spins and goes over to help Patricia at the bookcase. It's a full wall of books, so it could take a while.

"Is it going to matter now? You killed Jaxon, so you have no blood to operate the biometrics," I mutter, feeling devastated. A glint of metal catches my eye, a sharp letter opener on Dad's desk that they've both missed. I slowly move over to it, not wanting to move too fast and catch their attention. Picking it up, I slip it between my hands to hide it. If I get five minutes of peace, maybe I can cut through the cable ties.

Peter steps away from the bookcase. "Good point. We need the sister now. You keep going. Harlow and I are going to see if we can find her."

"Don't be silly. None of them are home. If they were, they would have already come to investigate. The two of you aren't exactly quiet," I argue with him, kicking myself for bringing it up. I have no clue if they are or aren't, but I don't want to risk that they're holed up somewhere.

He waves his gun at me, and I sigh defeatedly. He's going to make me no matter what I say. I'm really fucking sick of him and his fucking gun. I trudge out of the office, and when we get to the front of the house, I need to decide which wing to take him to. The boys are all gone, and hopefully Jacinta is smart enough not to be in there, so I choose their wing.

I walk slowly, taking him through the door to our wing. When I look around the entertainment area, I breathe a sigh of relief that she's not here, but Peter's eyes light up when he sees her bookcase.

"Naughty Harlow, you didn't tell me there was another bookcase here." He pushes me forward. My hands are hidden, so I start using the letter opener to saw away at my cable ties.

"It's full of Jacinta's smutty books. I very much doubt Dad would hide it here," I tell him, hoping to keep him distracted.

He pulls out a book and frowns, though I chuckle when I glance to see what he's holding. It's an MM omegaverse with two sexy man chests on the front. He throws it on the floor in disgust and continues to search.

Finally, I feel the plastic of the cable ties give before they drop away to the floor. I'm free, and I have a weapon in my hand. The anger that had been slowly bubbling away comes to a rolling boil, and I see red. I'm not going to wait and see if I get another chance to act. He's already killed someone I love. I won't take the risk that anyone else comes to harm.

I pull my arm back over my head, letter

opener at the ready, but just as I'm about to stab him, the door bursts open, and men with guns come pouring into the room. Peter whirls around, his gun pointing at them, so I lunge. A battle cry worthy of a valkyrie comes from my mouth as I plunge the letter opener into the side of his neck. A strangled scream is torn from his as he drops his gun and reaches for his neck, and when I yank the letter opener back out, I'm covered in blood spray. There's shouting and movement, but I have tunnel vision. I'm not about to let this man get away, so I stab again, screaming my fury, but an arm around my waist pulls me away.

I try to lash out at them until I recognize the uniform, managing to stop the downward move-ment just in time. I'm dragged away as Peter is surrounded by agents. There's shouting about medics and an ambulance, but I can tell by the way the blood is pumping and the amount of it covering the pale blue carpets that it's not going to make it on time—I hit his carotid artery. Immense satisfac-tion fills me as I watch the motherfucker bleed out. I'm passed from one set of arms to another, but I don't take my eyes off of him.

I want to watch him take his last breath, then I want to spit on his dead body.

Suddenly, I remember Patricia, and I gasp, struggling to get away from the arms holding me. "There's another one! She's in Dad's office," I shout, and the person holding onto me tightens his arms.

"Harlow, honey, it's okay. They already got her." Dad's voice finally penetrates my panic, and I slump in relief, knowing that I'm safe. The tears I had been holding back for so long start flowing, and I spin around in my dad's arms and hold him tight.

"Jaxon," I sob as he leads me away from Peter and the people trying to save him.

"What about Jaxon?" Jacinta asks, coming out of Dad's wing of the house, followed by Nana and Poppy. They all crowd around me as agents bring out a struggling Patricia. She's shouting and cursing, but the two agents have her under control.

As they pass us, I pull away from Dad and step in front of them. Cocking my fist back, I punch her square in the nose. The agents don't even stop me. Her head flies back on the impact, and I feel one of my knuckles collapse, sending pain shooting up my arm, but I refuse to show this woman any weakness. "I hope you end up some big butch woman's bitch when you get to prison, or even better, I hope you get shivved by a sharpened toothbrush and bleed to death all alone. It's what you deserve."

"You mean like your boyfriend did." She gives me a ghastly smile, the blood from her nose staining her teeth and making her look even more crazy than she is. The agents continue on out to a waiting car while she cackles madly the whole way. When I look back at my family, Poppy has his arms around

Jacinta, and she's looking at me like she can't believe what she just heard.

"Tell me she's talking about when Holden was shot. Please, Harlow!" she begs, but of course I can't, and she sees it in my eyes.

Poppy tightens his arms as she starts to struggle and scream. "Where is he? Where's my brother?" Both Nana and Dad are looking to me for information. I'm just about to tell them when one of the agents comes out of the room where Peter was, phone to his ear.

"Okay, Thomas, I'll let them know. Thank you."

"What did he say, Jake?" Dad demands.

"The guys checked out the cabin that was listed as Patricia's. It was obviously empty except they did find Jaxon." Jake looks at me with sympathy in his eyes before his gaze moves back to Jacinta. Tears are streaming down her face much like mine.

"He had been shot and was unconscious and unresponsive, but they did find a pulse. They flew him to the closest hospital, and he's in surgery. That's all they could tell me right now. They're currently waiting in Oliver's room."

"He's alive? I thought for sure he was dead. He tackled Peter, and the gun went off. There was so much blood!" I'm sobbing so hard the words are hard to understand. Jacinta breaks away from Poppy and runs to me. I brace for a hit, but she throws her arms around me and sobs with me instead.

"Oliver?" Nana asks.

"He donated blood on the trip in the chopper. He's currently recovering with a bag of saline and some juice. He got a bit lightheaded toward the end," Jake reports, and for the first time since I left Jaxon lying in a pool of blood, I have hope.

"Well, what are we waiting for? Jake, I'll leave you here. We have somewhere we need to be," Dad tells the agent, who says he'll speak to us when we've dealt with Jaxon.

Jacinta and I are bustled out the door by Dad and our grandparents, and before we know it, we're flying down the freeway in the direction of the hospital they're at. I'm sure the hospital staff are going to think *I* need treatment, what with Peter's blood splashed all over me. Ever prepared, Nana calmly passes me a couple of wet wipes from the glove box.

"It's not much, but it might help."

I wince when I reach out to grab one. The knuckles on my right hand are not feeling good at all. Maybe I will need them to look me over.

"I am so sorry," I say to Jazzy. She hasn't let go of my other hand since we got shoved into the back seat of the SUV, which is a positive sign, but I'm still feeling worried. Dad is driving like a bat out of hell while Poppy and Nana offer directions. I think they're deliberately leaving us alone for the moment.

"Harlow, none of this is your fault. If we have

to blame anyone, let's blame my biological grandpa. Seems to me that he was an evil fuckwit. It's because of him all of this is in play."

"Yeah, but it was my aunt who was the ringleader," I argue, which makes Nana turn around.

"Let's not do this to ourselves. The people who are to blame are dead or being punished. Let's look forward now. Once Jaxon is better, think about how much fun you're all going to have with your future plans for the house and the zoo." Even though Nana's trying to sound upbeat and positive, her eyes are still haunted. None of us will feel better until we reach the hospital and get updated.

The almost two-hour trip takes just over an hour and twenty. Dad ignores all speed limits to get there as quickly as possible, and luck must be on our side since we don't get pulled over by any highway cops. He finds the nearest parking spot, which isn't all that near due to our helicopter sitting in the parking lot.

Poppy chuckles, pointing to it as we all get out. "I bet that's going to cost us."

"Hush, Howard, it's totally worth it," Nana scolds as we rush across the blacktop and into the hospital.

It doesn't take us long to get directed to Oliver's room. When we arrive, I'm surrounded by my boyfriends, then kisses and hugs are exchanged and lots of prayers of thanks. But I push away from them and go over to check on Oliver.

"Have we heard anything about Jaxon?" I demand from my perch on his bed, looking at the others, but I can tell by their defeated looks that there's nothing to share. Nana and Poppy sit down, and the guys take turns telling us what happened.

Oliver has a hold of my hand and is not letting go. I'm happy to lean back against his chest, being careful of the drip in his arm, and listen to what they had been doing while I was traipsing through the tunnels.

It's about ten minutes later that a doctor walks in, his blue scrubs covered in blood. He pulls the mask off his face and looks around. Oliver's hand tightens in mine, and the hope that I had been holding on to disappears as he shakes his head.

"I'm so sorry…"

Chapter Twenty-Four

Harlow
Four weeks later.

The music is somber as the coffin lowers into the ground, and the smattering of people who had attended disperses. The open investigation had delayed it longer than we'd wanted, but it's finally done, and today we're able to put our family to rest.

"Are you ready?" Jaxon holds out his hand to me as I turn to look at him.

"Yeah, I am. Thanks for waiting for me." I take the offered hand, and we walk back to the limos where the rest of our family is standing. Jaxon had been released from the hospital a week ago with strict instructions to rest, but he insisted on coming to the funerals. He's still a little weak, so when we get to the cars, I push everyone out of the way and open the door, allowing him to slide in.

At my request, Cecelia, Raquel, and Luke have all been laid to rest in a family plot that Dad had purchased for them. Victims of their circumstances, it could have easily been me or Jax and Jacinta who had turned out like that. Well, maybe not if our fathers had been around. Our mothers, though, are another story.

Julia and Peter were cremated, and I told the funeral company to dump their ashes in the trash. I want nothing to do with them. They destroyed so many lives for nothing but their own selfish greed.

"Well, I'm glad that's done." Jacinta dusts off her hands like she was the one who had dug the graves instead of the cemetery workers. "I don't know about anyone else, but I am ready to party," she says to the rest of the crowd gathered around the limos. Despite her words, her voice is strained, and she hasn't lost the haunted look in her eyes that she's been wearing for weeks now.

Emma and Molly are both with Dad, as well as Chuck and Melinda. Hope, Alex, Shane, and Jace all showed up to lend their support too. Maxine is once again a no show, but I can't worry about her anymore. She's made her choice, and I'm afraid she's not only damaged our friendship. She's damaged her relationship with her parents, too, but she's a problem for another day.

Today is October thirty-first, and it's my and the

twins' birthdays. Having a triple funeral is probably not the best way to celebrate, but I didn't want to put it off any longer.

It was almost a quadruple funeral. When the doctor came into the room and apologized, we had all thought the worst. He was quick to set the record straight, though I still think his bedside manner needs some work. He was apologizing for taking so long to come and update us. Apparently, one of the hospital board members had reamed him out for keeping the Summers family waiting.

The bullet had punctured Jaxon's lung, and although he'd lost a lot of blood, Thomas' quick thinking and Oliver's blood kept him alive. They were able to remove the bullet and reinflate his lung, so he was going to be okay.

Fast forward to today, and the last thing I want to do is go out. While Jaxon was recovering in the hospital, the other guys had found a new mattress for my incredible bed in the panic room and started moving some of our stuff into the house. We're only using the safe room bedroom for now because so much of the rest of the house needs to be reno-vated and decorated, and that's going to take time. There are a couple of extra mattresses on the floor because although we can all fit on the bed, nobody wants to sleep in a pile of limbs. So they take turns rotating through my bed and crashing on the floor mattresses. All of us have a few outfits hung up in the wardrobe, and we make the trip back to Dad's as we need more. Every day, we have people coming in and out of the house, doing what needs to be done. Jacinta has been like a pig in mud managing all of that while I keep track of everything that's going on in the zoo. We have a long way to go before it's ready for occupation, but looking after Nyx and the cubs is enough for us right now.

"I'm sorry, but this year is going to be a quiet one for us," I announce, and Jacinta's bottom lip drops in a pout. "Don't let us stop you. Take Hope and have fun, but I've had enough excitement to last me a lifetime. We're crashing in our wing at Dad's place for a monster movie marathon, some popcorn, and pajamas."

Jacinta grumbles some more, but when I glance at each of my guys, none of them are disappointed. All of them agree with me about needing less excitement in our lives. Maybe once the zoo and our house and Jaxon's new cruise line are all running smoothly, we'll start needing some again, but by then we'll have a new life to care for. What else is more exciting than a baby?

I am not particularly thrilled at the arrangement Kai, Thomas, and Forrest came up with Veronica's doctors' help. The thought that we are going to be pandering to that bitch for the next four months makes me want to stab something... again. But I will grit my teeth and bear it for their sake because I know neither Kai nor Thomas want to be doing it either. I can't make it any harder for them than it already is.

Thanksgiving and Christmas are coming soon. The Summers have a Thanksgiving family tradition where they donate their time to the homeless and less fortunate. They turn one of Jaxon's clubs into a soup kitchen for the evening and give out food to people in need, so we have that coming up next month. It's our turn for Christmas this year, and Poppy decided that instead of having it in town, we all need a change of scenery. We're all going up to the cabin at Lake Superior and having a white Christmas with lots of food, wine, and winter activities. If some of those activities include snuggling by a fireplace with my boyfriends, I won't complain, but Kai is mad keen to go snowboarding, and I can't say his enthusiasm isn't infectious. Plus, I'll finally be meeting the infamous Aunt Merideth when she takes a trip across the pond to visit. She sounds like a wonderful woman, and I'm dying to meet her.

All in all, I'm looking forward to life settling down a bit, but I don't think that's really going to happen. I'm just glad that none of us have to look over our shoulders anymore. That feeling of always being watched is finally gone, so we are free to live our lives like they're supposed to be.

We part ways in the parking lot. Everyone is headed to the hotel for the night, giving me and the guys the run of the house this evening, but first

Thomas and Kai need to visit with Veronica. Today's her six-month prenatal scan, and while they're both excited to see the baby and learn about her progress, it's also wearing on them. They're making weekly visits to ensure she stays healthy and on track, and I know it's especially hard on Thomas. When he gets home from the visits, he heads directly to the shower and stays there for over half an hour trying to wash the feel of her off his skin.

I tried to insist on accompanying them today, but they both flatly refused. Kai was afraid that Veronica would see me and react negatively, which I guess is valid, but I can't stop the wave of jealousy that rolls over me. Then I feel guilty because I know neither of them want to be there either.

Once we get home, I change out of my funeral clothes, pulling on a pair of yoga pants and one of the guy's shirts. I think it's Kai's since there's some sports logo on it, but it's soft and comfortable, and that's all that matters.

I'm in desperate need of a distraction, or I'm going to stare at the clock nonstop until they get home. I head over to the big cat enclosure, excited to see how the cubs and Nyx are doing. I haven't had a chance to get in and see them for a few days.

Programming in the code on the keypad beside

the door, it clicks open, allowing me entry. The cubs have grown heaps in the last six weeks. They're roughly two months now, and they're starting to explore a lot more. They haven't been allowed out into the enclosure up until now,

but Clem and Doug are talking about allowing Nyx and them out together sometime this week. I think that will benefit all of them, and I'm excited to see it happen.

Nyx chuffs at me when she sees me, putting her paw up against the cage, which is how she's started greeting visitors. I rest my hand against hers on the other side of the wire.

"Hey, pretty girl. Everything okay?" I coo to her before grabbing a hunk of meat out of the fridge and tossing it into the cage through the feeding shoot. She drags it into a corner and starts gnawing on it while I open the door for the cub cage.

The cubs all pop their heads up at the sound of the door opening. They're still having bottled milk, but they've started on chopped meat too. There are a couple of bowls of it in the fridge, but I want them to get to room temperature first before I feed it to them. I don't want them to get upset tummies, so it has to warm up before they can try it.

One of them gets up and ambles over to me, so I take a seat on the ground. Daphne, the little cuddler, is happy to sit in my lap and let me stroke her. They all have collars on for now, identifying them, but they'll come off eventually.

Eventually, all the other cubs make their way over to me except Shaggy. That one really lives up to his name and will only come with food incentives. I've been there for about half an hour when I hear the outside door open again, then Declan appears.

"There you are. We were looking for you and were a little worried when we couldn't find you." There's a shadow in his eyes, and another wave of guilt flows through me.

"Fuck, Dec, I'm so sorry. I wasn't thinking. What with the funerals and worrying about Thomas and Kai and everything, I didn't think to tell you guys where I was going. That was insensitive of me."

He leans against the other side of the cage, and of course the cubs scramble away to run over to him. He crouches down at their level and sticks a finger through to rub their little heads, smiling widely.

He's been a little sad this week. His kittens all went to their new homes, and he decided to have Princess spayed too. At least she's been extra snuggly because she's been miserable after the operation so that has made up for him missing the kittens. It also means that he's been able to handle the cubs too. Princess has finally got used to the smell of them on him, so he's in full cat daddy mode, enjoying his time with all his favorite felines.

"It's understandable. You've been through so

much in such a short amount of time," he says kindly. "And the Veronica situation is not an easy one to live with."

I stand up, brushing fur off myself before going over to join him at the wall of the cage. "No, it's not, but I don't want to make things more difficult for Kai and Thomas, so I'll keep my insecurities to myself," I tell him, then point to the bowls on the bench. "Can you pass me those? I'll feed the guys, then we could go for a walk. If I'm not distracted, I'm just going to worry about them."

Together, we take care of the cubs until everyone is happily munching.

"Come on. I have something I want to show you." Declan grabs me by the hand and drags me away from the animals. Closing the door behind us, he activates the lock and drags me in the direction of the stables.

"Where are we going? I don't think Prada and Coco will appreciate us smelling like the big cats," I point out as he drags me around the house and across the helicopter landing pad to the stables.

"You'll see. Don't worry about the horses," he says mysteriously.

Inside, instead of leading me to the horses, he breezes straight past them to the big door that opens into the arena. But then he takes a left and opens another door I hadn't seen before. It leads to a set of stairs that brings us up to the hayloft at the top.

Laid out in a corner is a makeshift bed, with a wrapped gift sitting on top of it as well as a cupcake with an electric candle flickering in it. "What is this?" I ask my smug boyfriend.

"I know we're celebrating your birthday with everyone tonight, but I wanted to steal you away for a moment so I could give you the gift I got you." He pulls me across the bales of hay and drags me down into his little nest.

"Happy birthday, gorgeous." He holds out the present, as excited as a kid at Christmas.

"Thank you." I take it from him, unable to deny my own excitement. I've started to unwrap it when he starts talking again.

"I guess this is partly for you and partly for our future kids." It's all I can do to stop myself from running my hand across my belly with that comment. "Although this is happening much earlier than we thought it would, and she's not going to need it for a few years yet, I decided we needed another business for them to learn from like all of us did. I know you mentioned cleaning cages will be character building, but your love of abandoned buildings inspired me, and when my real estate agent sent me this, I knew it was fate."

When I open the package, I find a bundle of photos and a gorgeous metal bookmark that has a carousel at the top with zoo animals running along its length.

"This is gorgeous, Dec! I can't wait to use it in

my book." I put the bookmark to the side and flick through the photos, my heart starting to beat a little faster at what I'm seeing. "What exactly am I looking at?" I ask, wanting him to confirm my thoughts.

"We bought an amusement park. I went out and had a look at it last week. Some of it is run down and needs work, but things like that carousel there..." He points to the picture I'm currently stuck on. It's this gorgeous, pristine carousel with beautiful brightly painted wooden animals for riding on. "Are almost brand new. I thought we could start Neighpalm Amusements for our children."

If I wasn't completely in love with this man already, then this would have been the final nail in the coffin. I throw the picture to the side and launch myself at him, narrowly missing the cupcake. My lips slam against his in a clash of teeth and tongues, showing him just how much I like my birthday present.

Chapter Twenty-Five

Harlow

He pushes me away for a moment, moving the cupcake, photos, and bookmark to the side before pressing me back against the blankets and stripping me of my t-shirt and pants, leaving me lying there in just my panties. He runs a finger over my bare skin, circling my nipples before trailing it downward. I shiver as he lifts the edge of my panties, dragging them down my legs until I'm completely naked to his gaze.

A small smile on his lips has my own turning up as he pulls his shirt over his head before standing up and shucking off his shorts so that he's as naked as I am. Fisting his thick length, he kneels down next to me and runs his tongue through my folds without any hesitation. I flinch at the contact, but he uses his hands to hold my hips in place as he devours my pussy. The noises from my mouth are *not* quiet, and I pray that they can't be heard in the employee accommodation.

It's not long before Declan has me worked into a frenzy, and I'm a squirming, pleading mess. "Please, Dec. I need you." I tug on his hair until his mouth leaves my core and travels up, placing little kisses all the way up my body. He lines himself up and slams home in one quick movement, both of us groaning with pleasure.

"Fuck, you feel so tight. I love how your cunt squeezes my cock," he mutters in a low rumble as he takes a moment to bask in the sensations. But that's all he takes.

Pulling back, he sets a furious pace, hitching my leg over his hip to grind deep, hitting all the spots that make me call out his name. Both of us are panting and sweaty as I feel my orgasm just out of reach. I slide a hand in between us to flick my clit, and that's enough to send me over.

"God, I'm coming!" I shout as the waves of pleasure rush out from my center, sending shock-waves through my body.

"No, baby, not god, just Dec." He grits his teeth as he fucks me through my orgasm, then he stills, and I feel his dick pulsing as he cums deep inside me. "God, that feels so fucking good." He moans, sending residual pleasure through me as he grinds against my clit. His body slowly starts to relax, but I tightly wrap my legs around his hips when he goes to shift away from me.

"Please stay for a moment. I like the feel of your weight against my body." He stays put, and I nuzzle my face into his shoulder. His hair is getting long, and it tickles my face as I place little kisses against his neck, rubbing my hands up and down his body. I can still feel his cock throbbing inside of me, though soon enough, he's pulling away. I feel his cum slide out of me as he does, and there's a part of me that mourns its loss.

He rolls onto his back and pulls me against him. "So I take it you like it?" he asks, sounding almost hesitant, and I chuckle, pulling away to prop myself up so I can see him.

"Dec, I love it. It's amazing! I can't believe you did this. Thank you."

I lean in to kiss him again, but a sound catches my ear, making us both stop. It's the sound of an approaching helicopter. Dec sighs and stands up, tugging me up with him and passing over my discarded clothes.

"Come on. Kai and Thomas are going to need you." We dress quietly, our time now overshadowed by his brothers' impending arrival. Not because they're here, but because we know what kind of mood they'll be in after being forced to play happy family with Veronica.

By the time Dec and I gather up the blankets and my present, the helicopter has landed. Kai is the only one around as we walk across the landing strip while the rotor blades wind down.

"I'll take these and put them in your bedroom." Dec takes the photos and my bookmark from me and gives me a kiss. "I'll see you tonight if I don't see you before."

We part ways, and I wait as Kai climbs down from the cockpit, a wide grin on his face. My eyebrows raise in surprise. I was expecting a morose and depressed Kai, so this is a welcome surprise.

"Harlow, hi!" He waves his hand, which has something in it, before reaching back into the helicopter to pull out a gift bag.

He points at the patio and waves for me to keep going, so I leave him to lock up the helicopter while I take a seat at the outdoor table, which is surprisingly set for two, with another couple of cupcakes and two mugs of coffee. I'm taking a sip of one when Kai comes bounding across the patio to give me a quick kiss on the lips, leaving me breathless, before he takes a seat at the other setting.

"Hi. I had Mrs. Heyton set this up so we could talk while I gave you your birthday present."

"You're awfully cheerful. I guess the appointment went well, then?" I ask as he spreads his things out before taking a sip of his coffee. He scrunches up his nose in this really cute way before shrugging.

"Meh, Veronica was as manipulative as she always is, but Tom cops the brunt of that. She basically ignores me, so I got to ask all the questions I wanted about the baby. Look." He passes me a sheaf of photo printouts, and my heart lurches as I catch sight of what it is. There on the paper, perfectly formed, is Kai's baby, curled up all happy and snug in its home for the next three months. A tear slides down my face before I can stop it, but his finger catches it.

"Oh honey, I'm sorry. I know how hard this must be for you." He takes the papers from me and pulls me into his lap. "But I hope you know that I see this baby as *ours*. As far as I'm concerned, Veronica is no different than a surrogate helping out a family." He holds me tight as a shudder washes over me, but then I get a hold of my emotions.

"I know. I really do. I don't hold this against you or the baby, but I do have moments where I want to stab the bitch. You'll have to be patient with me. Once that baby is in my arms and we no longer have anything to do with her, I'll be happy. Half of what upsets me is the shit she puts you guys through. The fact that Tom has to take her something every time to appease her drives me wild. What was it today?" I ask as I try to pull myself out of his lap, but he's having nothing of it.

"A bracelet his PA picked out. He hasn't put any personal thought into anything she's been getting. He's trying to stay as impersonal as possible even though I know it's wearing on him. I'm worried about him, honestly."

I look through the glass door, but Tom is nowhere to be seen. I didn't think he would be, but being able to catch a glimpse of him would make me feel better. I'm about to suggest I check on him, but Kai beats me to it.

"Go and check on him, but before you do, I wanted to give you my present. It's nothing fancy, but I hope you know how much this means to me." He hands over a gift bag, and I pull out a book. *Name Your Baby.* "I want you to pick our daughter's name. I don't think she should be named after anyone. Neither of us have any biological family to name her after except Nana, but she's one of a kind, and I'm sure our daughter will be too, so I want her to have a unique name."

I'm speechless. I know Kai already considers me his daughter's mother, but until now, I hadn't truly allowed myself to get too attached. "Really?" I ask, still blown away by this.

"Yes, really. Have a look at what else is in the bag." I put the book down and pull out the other two items. This time, a wide smile creeps across my face as I see what he's given us. There in bright red and yellow are Neighpalm Shockwave jerseys, one obviously meant for me and one teeny-tiny baby-sized jersey. On the back of the big one is written Mama Summers. Then the little one has Baby Summers on it.

Aw, this guy is so fucking sweet, and he's not even done yet. He pulls out two shoe boxes and opens them up to reveal matching ice skates. I start to giggle uncontrollably.

"These are awesome, Kai. I can't wait to teach our daughter to skate." I lean in and press a kiss against his cheek.

"Hey, maybe we'll build an indoor rink on the property. Then you won't have to go anywhere else to do it," he suggests as I stand up.

"Leave it to you guys to do something like that. Let's get the zoo finished before we think about that." My attempt to curb his enthusiasm goes completely unnoticed. Yep, I've already lost him.

"I'm sure Dad would let us build it on here. Then Jacinta and Hope's future kids can use it too. I'm going to send Miles a message, get him looking at this." He pulls his phone out of his pocket and swipes his fingers across the screen.

"Okay, before you get lost, I'm going to say thank you for these. I'll take them upstairs and check on Tom while I'm up there." He absently waves at me, already plotting as I look wistfully at the cupcakes. *Maybe I'll get to eat one eventually.* Sighing, I grab all my gorgeous things and take them inside. No point in taking them up to my room, really, when it's all going to have to go over to our place anyway. I leave them on a side table in the foyer, so I won't forget to take them when we leave.

Our wing is quiet as I trudge up the stairs. I know Jax was taking a nap when we got back from the funerals, and I can hear murmuring in Holden's room as I walk past it on the way to Tom's. I'll poke my head in and check on them a little later.

The door to Thomas' room is cracked open, so I slide through it. The room is dark, his drapes still closed across the windows. The only light is shining from a crack in the bathroom door. Stripping down, I leave my clothes on the floor in his room and slowly open up the bathroom door. The room is full of steam, and the glass to the shower is all fogged up. Even if it wasn't, I'm not sure Thomas would have noticed me. He's leaning both hands against a wall, his head down, as hot water rushes over his body. He's so lost in his mind that he hasn't even heard me yet, which is telling. He's always so alert.

Sliding the door open, I step in as Thomas whirls around at the sound. When he sees it's me, he slumps once more, so I gather him into my arms and hold him tight. He tries to struggle and push me away, but I'm like an octopus holding on tight. My face pushes against the tattoo spread out across his chest.

"I don't deserve you. I feel like I'm cheating on you every time I visit that woman," Thomas mutters, sounding destroyed. I don't think I've ever heard him like this, not even when both of his brothers were shot. He's like a shell of a man.

"Now, stop that," I scold him, shaking my head. "We all know you're doing the best thing for our daughter, just as you would for any of us. No one holds that against you. I'm just sorry you have to go through it. Soon enough, she will be here, and you'll hold her in your arms. When that moment comes, everything that has occurred will pale in significance to the wonder of new life. It will all be worth it."

I feel him shudder as I run my hands over his back in small comforting strokes. We just stand there, letting the water wash away our worries. Finally, he pulls away and looks down at me. "I'm sorry. It's your birthday, and I'm bringing it down."

"Pretty sure the three funerals this morning did that. I'm just enjoying spending time with you all. It feels like ages since I've had a moment to breathe and just be with you guys."

"Well, I can't give you your present until after we get out of the shower, so how about we do that?" he says, trying to step around me, but I block him.

"And how about I make you forget all about what you did today? I know you. You're going to get out, then it will all come rushing back. I'd rather give you something else to think about." I drop to my knees and take his length in my hand, loving the way it starts to harden as I lick the drops of water from it. He's lost the defeated look in his eyes, and it's been replaced by desire. Now, that's what I like to see.

I take him deep into the back of my throat with hardly any lead up, and he grunts, his hand threading through my wet hair. I want to make it fast and hard, so it doesn't leave him any time to think. Cupping his balls with my other hand, I roll them as I bob up and down, hollowing my cheeks and sucking. Sliding my finger back, I press into his tight hole until his knees buckle.

"Oh shit, Harlow." His voice is ragged as I search for the sensitive spot inside his channel. Once I rub against it, it's not long before his hands tighten. "I'm going to cum," he warns, but I just continue to give him pleasure. I want him to lose his mind and forget about earlier. He takes over, thrusting back and forth as he holds my head still. My gag reflex protests. Tears stream down my face, and spit runs out the side of my mouth, but the water just washes it away.

Finally, he stills, and I feel the hot rush of his cum at the back of my throat and taste his salty flavor. Swallowing him down, I wait for him to stop before pushing him away. I run my tongue over the eye of his dick, catching the last of his essence, before standing up. I catch some water in my mouth as he leans his head on my shoulder, panting. His hands cup my ass and pull me against him, his still hard length trapped between us. He takes my mouth with his and slowly devours it, tasting and licking as he thrusts his knee between my legs, allowing me to grind against it.

"Your turn," he says as he pulls away, pushing me against the wall and dropping to his knees.

"I'm not going to argue with that," I tell him, leaning back against the wall as he takes my hips in his hands and dives in.

Chapter Twenty-Six

Harlow

Once we've finished, I leave Thomas to get dressed and head downstairs, but as I pass Holden's room, I hear him call out to me.

"Harlow, can you come in here a moment?"

I step into his room and look around. "Hey, what happened to Oli? I thought I heard the two of you talking before." Holden smirks and raises an eyebrow.

"We heard that you were upstairs, so I asked him to give us a moment." I blush at how they may have heard me. I wasn't quiet, and after Thomas had finished eating me out, he'd fucked me hard against the shower wall. "It sounds like your birthday is starting to get good."

I roll my eyes and take a seat on the bed next to

him, but he's not happy to let me stay there. He tugs me into his arms, giving me a long lingering kiss before pulling away.

"Hi." He's smiling after leaving me breathless.

"Hi yourself," I whisper back once I recover my voice.

"We haven't had much quality time together since the kidnapping and Jaxon's shooting. All of us have been so busy with catching up on work and the house and zoo renovations, but I took some time last week and had a look at the library. Although it's full of books, I was fairly certain it wasn't going to be the kind of books that we wanted to have in our library, and I was right. Most of them are in Romanian and aren't particularly interesting, so I made arrangements to donate them to a Romanian community in New York."

He reaches to the side of his bed, grabbing a small gift that he hands out to me. "Happy birthday, Mistress." He winks and smiles as I roll my eyes, laughing.

I take it from him and tear open the paper. Inside is a brand new reverse harem novel that I haven't read before—*Manix* by Grace McGinty. I flip it over and read the blurb, which sounds awesome, and now I can't wait to dive in. Out of it tumbles a piece of paper, and when I pick it up and read it, my mouth drops open. It's a voucher to one of the biggest bookstores in LA for twenty grand.

"I figured that would help you start filling the

shelves. They're happy to order in any indie authors you may want. I remember you saying you like to support the smaller less-well-known ones. Jacinta helped me pick that one out."

My heart fills. How did all of these men pick such perfect gifts? Each one is a way of connecting us, showing that they care about what's important to me.

"This is amazing, thank you! I can't wait to make a list of all the books I want. Oh, and I want to get some nonfiction and some children's books, too. Its never too soon to start introducing a love of books to children. I can't wait to read to our daughter." His hand rests on my stomach, and a wave of butterflies tickles me inside. He gives me a squeeze before he shoves me off the bed, and I can't help the shout that escapes as I try not to hit the ground.

Hands on my hips, I glare at him. "What the fuck?"

"Sorry. I have instructions to send you down to the garage. Jaxon is waiting there for you. We better not keep him waiting, He's still not moving too fast, and I don't want him on his feet for too long. I'll walk with you."

He takes the hand that isn't occupied and escorts me downstairs, leaving me at the door that leads to the garage with a kiss.

"When you're done here, we're meeting back in the common area of our wing for movies. I'm going to order us some food." With that, he walks away, and I place his gift beside the one from Kai before opening the garage door.

The lights are on, and I can see Jaxon on the other side next to where he keeps his bike. He looks up and waves when I enter.

"Hey, sweetie, come over here for me, will you?"

I move around the parked cars, a prick of worry niggling at my mind. Jaxon sounds tired. I'm going to force him to sit down when we're done here.

When I get to him, he's standing next to something covered in a black sheet. "Happy birthday. Tada!" He pulls the sheet aside, wincing with the movement.

"Jaxon, be careful," I scold him, but my attention is quickly caught on what he revealed. Under the sheet is a brand-new, shiny eggplant purple Suzuki Hayabusa, with a matching helmet and black bike leathers sitting on its seat.

"Oh my god. Is this for me?" I ask him, running a hand over the cold metal and leather seat. He's beaming when my gaze moves away from the sexy machine and back to him.

"Yup, now we can go for rides together." But then his face falls as he runs a hand through my hair. "Crap, I think I fucked up. Now I won't have you riding behind me, pressing your delicious body against mine."

I laugh and gently wrap my arms around him.

He's mostly healed, but I know things still ache. "Don't worry. I'm sure we can still do that too. Thank you. I love it and can't wait to take it for a spin. I have something for you as well, but it's in my backpack upstairs. How about we head inside? You get comfortable on the couch while I run upstairs and get it."

"You have something for me?" he asks, sounding surprised but pleased.

"Of course, silly. I have something for Jazzy too, but we'll have to give it to her another day."

We head back inside, and I leave him getting comfortable while I get his present. We chose to do movie night at Dad's because the theater at our place most definitely needs an upgrade.

I pick up Jaxon's present and carry it downstairs. When I get to the common area, I stop and look down at where Peter's blood had stained the carpet. I had wanted to keep it to memorialize that bastard's death and my hand in it, but I was outvoted by Jacinta who told me it was all hers now so there was no way we were leaving it. The carpet was replaced, but Declan made a deal with the carpet layers. When they removed the old one, they cut out the blood patch and gave it to him. He had it preserved somehow and framed, so it's hanging up in our office at our new place.

Holden got sick of us all calling it the count's and decided the estate needed a name. Kind of like Tara from *Gone with the Wind*. It took him a while to come up with something we all liked, but he finally did—Willow Castle. He had a lovely sign built, and it now graces the front gates.

Sighing, I step over where I know the patch was since it feels kind of wrong to step on it. I'm the first to arrive, so I make myself comfortable on the couch next to Jaxon.

It's not long before the other guys join us, making themselves comfortable, except Oli.

"What are you doing?" I ask him, a little suspicious of the grin on his face.

"Time for my present." He claps his hands like a child.

"We don't do presents for one another anymore," Holden explains to me. "So Oli is super excited about the fact that we can get them for you."

I struggle to sit up and shake my head. "You all know you didn't have to get me things. " A hand over my mouth stops my argument.

"Sit back, babe. We all definitely wanted to do this for you," Kai says as I gently shove Jaxon's hand away.

"We don't do it for each other because we have enough money to buy ourselves what we want, but we still love to spoil Nana, Jacinta, Hope, and Mrs. H on their birthdays. We'll probably do the same for Emma and Molly too now that they're in our lives," Declan explains.

"Go and get the thing, Oli." Thomas chuckles

as his brother does a little dance on the spot like he needs to pee and can't control his enthusiasm. Oli runs away as Jaxon strokes his hand over my head.

"Shall I give you yours while we wait?" I ask him, but before he can say anything else, Oli returns, and he's carrying a saddle. I sit up straight with excitement. It's a beautiful black leather English saddle that looks like it's made from the finest of leather.

"Wow!" The exclamation slips out as I slide my butt forward on the sofa so I can get a better look as he lays it at my feet. "It's beautiful. Thank you so much." I run my hands over the pommel and down the seat, loving that it's as soft as it looks. "Why is this so familiar, though? I feel like I've seen it before."

"You have. Alex told me about it when I was lamenting about what to give you. It's the saddle from your first shopping trip with him when you arrived in LA. I thought it was a good idea considering what Thomas got you." Oli's still vibrating like a guitar string with excitement, but the others are looking more relaxed than I've seen them for a while. The stress of the stalker really had been piling up. Having this quiet downtime with just the seven of us has been magic.

I then realize what Oli said. "Thomas?" I ask, unable to hide my curiosity.

He gets up and goes over to the bookshelf and pulls out a folder. When he comes back, the other four crowd around me and Jaxon as he hands it over.

"I know how much you love Sampson, but he's Chuck's horse, and he's booked up for ages with movies. With his contacts, he helped me find you a replacement."

My happiness growing, I open up the folder. In it is a picture of a black friesian foal. He's six months old and has recently been weaned from his mom, and the paperwork says he's being delivered in two days. A gasp escapes my lips as I look over the paperwork. It shows *my* name, Harlow Summers, as the registered owner. This little guy is all mine.

Thomas grunts as I slam my body into him, plastering kisses all over his face before moving through the rest of the guys. They're all smiling like they've won the lottery, and by the time I get to Jaxon, I'm more careful but no less enthusiastic with him.

"Thank you so much. This is a dream come true! Thank you for all your wonderful gifts," I tell them.

"Chuck told us it was, and we would be bad boyfriends if we didn't at least make that dream come true," Thomas replies as Oli scoffs.

"Please, her dreams come true every time I get naked and fu—" He breaks off when Holden elbows him in the side.

"Now, we know the saddle isn't going to fit him

for a while, so I have a heap of other gear for him too. I think Jacinta bought two of everything when she went shopping for Coco."

Leaning back, I sigh with happiness, but something stabs me in the side. "Oh yeah, Jaxon's present." I put the folder to the side and pick up the little gift, holding it out to him. My other hand is hidden behind my back, fingers crossed that this winds up being a good surprise.

He takes the gift and quickly unwraps it, a frown coming across his face as he tries to work out what it is. He rolls it over, and the furrows between his brows deepen. The butterflies in my stomach become birds of prey as I wait for his response.

"Well, what the fuck is it?" Oliver demands, trying to get a look, but Holden holds him back.

Suddenly, Jaxon's eyes widen. "No?" he gasps, and I shrug sheepishly.

"Happy birthday! Who would have thought that evil bastard would actually get something right?"

Jaxon lunges at me and pulls me against him, too tight for his wounds, of course, but at the moment he doesn't seem to care. A smile crosses my lips as he whispers promises of love and support.

"But what is it?" Oliver asks again, a slight whine to his tone, and Jaxon and I crack up laughing.

Life is going to be pretty fucking great.

The motherfucking end....
For now

Thank you for reading!
I hope you enjoyed the book. It would be super awesome if you could leave a review wherever you bought it, because I love to hear what you thought of the story.

Not sick of the Neighpalm Industries world yet?
Well, don't despair Jacinta's story will be coming out next.
Pre-order Superficial Girl here

Want to keep up to date with new books coming soon? Sign up to my newsletter here
Newsletter

Another way to do that is to join me Facebook group. I drop teasers and giveaways in there all the time. Here's the link
Lexie's Ladygarden

Visit my webpage and check out reading orders and what else I've written.
www.lexiewinston.com

Acknowledgments

Well, we're done! I don't know about you but I'm feeling slightly emotional. We're finally at the end of that rollercoaster of a ride.

When I started this book I had two covers and one was going to be Harlow's story and the other was going to be Jacinta's. I knew even before I was half way through Abandoned Girl that this was going to blow out but I never thought it would be six books worth or that it would get the reception it did. Thank you to each and every one of you that has stuck with me and Harlow for this journey. I just hope that you stick around and find out what's going on with Max and see if Hope and Jacinta get their happy endings too.

Thank you to all the normal crew this book wouldn't be possible without you all.

Thank you.....

Michelle for your invaluable editing.

Emma for all the late night and early morning chats.

Breakout Designs for the cover.

Kerry and Jillian you keep the words flowing with your commentary and support.

My beta team for being super awesome as usual.

Leslie Arnett, for your professional veterinarian knowledge. I'd be lost without you.

Grace and Hope for being my emotional support humans and talking me down from every angst ridden ledge I'v been on.

Thank you to everyone who reviews and recommends it and thank you to all of you who take the chance and preorder the next one as soon as you've finished the last. You guys are the reason I can keep writing this story.
Until next time. Happy Reading
Xoxo

Lexie

Check out something else by me. Dark Poly Romance with both MM and FF and was as many possible triggers. Make sure you read the trigger warning at the front.

Secrets Kept

Broken Promises Series

I wasn't always like this you know. I used to be one of those girls who was bubbly and people thought sunshine came out of my ass. That is until my best friend kissed me and then betrayed me with those same lips. I became ridiculed and bullied and my soul slowly died inside until I was a shadow of my former self.

But then my father introduced me and my brother to our family legacy and I became glad of the fractured, broken soul I'd become. In fact, I reveled in it. We trust no one but each other, blood is always thicker than water. Heaven help those that betray us. Because we aren't afraid to get our hands dirty.

This book is a mafia dark poly romance. There will be MM and FF and various combinations. It will contain sexual situations that may make you feel uncomfortable. There will be drugs references and violence. Please read the content at the beginning for a more concise list of possible triggers. You have been warned

Get it now